LUCKY BOY

By
Cameron Morfit

Copyright © 2016

Editorial Work by AnnaMarie McHargue

Cover Design by Arthur Cherry

Interior Design by Aaron Snethen

Published in Boise, Idaho by Elevate Fiction, a division of Elevate Publishing.

Web: www.elevatepub.com

For information please email info@elevatepub.com

ISBN (print): 9780996465502

ISBN (e-book): 978-0-9964655-1-9

Printed in the United States of America.

For Grandma

ENDORSEMENTS

"Morfit's coming-of-age novel evokes Tom Sawyer, except that it's set in modern-day Boise, Idaho, and the Huck Finn role is played by a chain-smoking, 33-year-old tow-truck driver/golf coach who believes in talismans and bio-harmonic convergence. Mark Twain, if he were alive, would happily pay for his copy."

— **John Garrity**
Contributing Writer at *Sports Illustrated*
Author of *Ancestral Links*, *Tiger 2.0*, and *Tour Tempo*

"There's more than one way to enjoy a book as good as *Lucky Boy*. You can certainly lose yourself in the golf, and it's even better as the story of an unlikely friendship between two very different souls. More than that, though, Cameron Morfit accomplishes a feat that doesn't come easy to adults, whether they're writers, or teachers, or even parents—he actually remembers what it was like to be young. He remembers the paralyzing anxiety, and the intense passions, and the small moments of redemption that help to define our budding senses of self. He understands that there are no villains in these confusing years, only people trying to find their place, and that knowledge informs every word on every page. How can you forget someone like Max, or Sadie, or Dewey, when they're so full of humanity? Morfit writes with the kind of empathy—for all his characters—that you just can't fake."

— **Shane Ryan**
New York Times Bestselling Author of *Slaying The Tiger*

"Luck, love, golf and high school. Throw in a surprising twist and a dash of Groundhog Day and you have the winning coming-of-age tale, *Lucky Boy*, deftly told by Cameron Morfit."

— **Don Brown**
Author of *Drowned City*, *The Train Jumpers*, and *The Notorious Izzy Fink*

CHAPTER 1

Eighth grade started predictably for Max Buras.

His mother took him to Ross Dress For Less to restock his collection of shirts—mostly short-sleeved, button-down, collared. She always did.

She took him to Office Depot for a new binder and some paper and pens, and a template for Gabe for his parallelograms. And she always shopped there, as well.

At school, Max couldn't remember his locker number and wrote it on a slip of paper he kept in his backpack. He got into auto shop. Missy McGrath had lost her braces and turned stunningly beautiful. Susannah Jurevicious was still beautiful. And the single-story, mostly brick Bridge Academy, across from the library, had gotten a fresh coat of paint—still beige with brown trim and black window lintels. Boise, Idaho, a medium-sized town nestled amid the rumpled foothills, was as hot as usual for late summer.

Predictable.

It was a hot Friday afternoon, and Max's shirt stuck to his back as he pedaled home from school. His older sister was already there; she must have gotten a ride.

With two weeks in the books, they only had—what, another 35 or so before summer vacation? It was all too depressing to think about. In his room Max let his backpack drop to the floor with a thud before peeling off his shirt and putting on a fresh one. He flopped onto his bed and nearly onto an abandoned worksheet from two nights before—a science assignment he hadn't felt like doing, then or now.

The doorbell rang.

"Max!" Sadie yelled.

"Argh," Max said.

He was lying facedown on his bed, the magnifying glass in his hand redirecting the sunlight coming through his window. The sunlight was coalescing into a tiny, extremely concentrated laser beam of white-hot awesomeness onto the sheet of paper on the bed.

The goal, Max told himself, was merely to threaten to set his science homework ablaze, not to actually do it.

"Max! Someone at the door for you!"

Max pursed his lips and felt the late summer heat creep up the back of his neck, through his ginger, buzz haircut and up into the pinkish, lightly freckled pudginess of his cheeks. Although they needed no adjusting (they almost never did) he adjusted his glasses and their blue-black strap—stretchy and waterproof—that hugged his skull. He admired the black burn dots and the sliver of sweet-smelling smoke that wafted from his science homework before dropping it onto his desk.

"Max!"

"Alright, already, I'm coming! Geez. Have a cow, why don't you."

Off the bed, out the door to his room, down the mustard-colored hallway past all those framed black and white photos of himself and Sadie and Gabe, like they were old Hollywood stars. (Sadie was the family's only star amid Bridge Academy's complicated social hierarchy.)

"Coming," Max repeated.

In the kitchen he saw Gabe sitting atop a stool before a pile of gingersnaps, a glass of milk and his drawings. He hummed and rocked, gaping at the front door.

"Hey, Gabe!" Max said, stealing a cookie.

Gabe gave no reply. (He never did.)

Sadie was gripping both sides of the doorframe so Max could only see her back, in a blousy white shirt with zigzag black lines, and the silhouette of an adult on the other side of the threshold. She eyed Max behind her and lowered one of her arms.

Standing at the door was a tall, slender man with a pink, shiny face and buggy eyes. He wore beat up jeans, a yellow button-down, short-sleeved shirt, and an orange tie. His gigantic, canvas, high-top shoes had once been white but were now soiled with grease and grime.

Max felt Sadie looking at her brother for an explanation, but he didn't have one. He couldn't imagine a reason for the sudden and unannounced arrival of Uncle Dewey from Oregon.

"Uh," Dewey said, looking over Max's shoulder. "I think something might be burning."

CHAPTER 2

"Well, that was exciting. Afternoon! Dewey Tomlinson!" He shot his arm out and smiled to reveal a set of brown, unruly teeth, gapped in odd ways like a withering old ear of corn that's been picked at and finally abandoned.

Max felt the cooling sweat at the nape of his neck. His room smelled of smoke, but oddly the smoke alarms hadn't gone off—he would have to mention to his father that they needed new batteries. He appraised the small pile of ash on his desk, which was all that was left of the small fire he had accidentally sparked with his magnifying glass and his science homework, somehow setting his entire binder ablaze while he walked to the front door.

Dewey had sprinted down the hall with Max and Sadie trailing behind before climbing up onto the desk to stomp out the flames.

"We've met before," Dewey said, pumping Max's arm, "but I don't believe I've had the honor of meeting your sister."

"Dewey Tomlinson!" Dewey said, thrusting his hand toward her now.

"Uh, okay," Sadie said. She shrugged. They shook. "Sadie Buras!"

"Thanks, by the way," Max said. "For, um, putting out the fire."

"Shoes are black, anyway," Dewey said, looking down at his feet. "I'd say I'm about due for a new pair." He looked up again. "Anyone ever tell you not to play with fire?"

"Yeah," Max said, appraising the mess at his desk. He was going to need an extension on his science assignment. "Mom and Dad aren't going to like this."

"Oh, I don't think we have to tell Mom and Dad," Dewey said. "It'll be our secret."

"My binder," Max said.

"Tell you what," Dewey said, "I'll buy you a new one."

"I guess it's out now," Sadie said. "C'mon, let's go outside. It stinks in here. Open a window."

Max slid open the window next to his bed as far as it would go, and caught up to Dewey and Sadie as they made their way back down the hallway and out through the front door.

Theirs was a mid-century ranch house, single level, shaped like so many others of that style. At the end of the hallway, to the left, was the living room, with its built-in bookshelves, wood-burning fireplace and huge windows looking out onto the street. The room's most prominent feature was a large leather seat shaped like a baseball mitt, which no one ever sat in twice. The Boise Braves had given it to Max's sportswriter father after he left the baseball beat, and every day or two Max's mother talked longingly of the day they might get rid of it.

Gabe, unmoved by the all the excitement, was still seated in the kitchen, drawing, rocking a little in his seat. But his eyes locked onto the stranger in their midst. Gabe had never met him either. Only Max had; he'd "had a cup of coffee" with Dewey a year or so earlier, when Max and his mother had stopped in Pendleton on their way to the Oregon coast when his mom had taken "a much-needed getaway." Max had actually had a glass of milk; Dewey had made his mother a cup of instant "for the road."

The only other thing Max remembered was that Dewey had fed a saucer of milk to a cat that he said wasn't his but seemed to keep showing up at his door. Also, he kept calling himself "the black sheep" of the family. Dewey's foster mother was Max's mom's sister, or something. Max supposed that made him and Dewey cousins, or Max's mother and Dewey cousins. Somehow, though, the man from Pendleton had become "Uncle Dewey."

Still, he was a stranger to Sadie, who had stayed home with their dad and Gabe that weekend, since Sadie had had a show or a rehearsal. (*Theater Arts*, she always told Max, was the road to popularity.)

Max felt Gabe's eyes on them as he, Sadie and Dewey made it back to the front door and stepped back out into the light.

"You called for a tow truck?" Dewey craned his neck to indicate a shiny truck in front of the house, an enormous, metallic-blue rig with an orange-yellow-black decal on the side door—SONNY'S TOWING.

"Um…no?" Max said. "I don't think so?"

"Aw, I'm just kiddin'," Dewey said. He scratched behind his ear, stroked his goatee. "Your mom here?"

"She's not home yet," Max said, relieved to finally know the answer.

"Huh," Dewey said again.

Max looked at Dewey's dirty fingernails. His face was drawn in and gaunt, with deep-set, hollow eyes, his skin a bluish burgundy.

"So, uh," Max mumbled.

Sadie turned to go back down the hallway. "I'll be in my room if you need me. I've got homework. Don't let all the heat in."

"Okay," Max said, maintaining eye contact with Dewey. He listened for the sound of her door closing, but didn't hear it.

"You look like you might want a look at that truck," Dewey said.

Max's stomach jumped. "Me? No. Well, uh, I don't know. I mean, not really."

"Why don't you come on out here and I'll show it to you?"

Oh, gawd. *Come see my truck.* What a terrible idea. "Okay," Max said as he shrugged his assent. He slipped his flip-flops on, closed the front door and followed Dewey to the street.

"We won't go any place," Dewey said. "I'll just show you how it works, see? You don't see a rig like this every day. Or, if you do, you're monthly tow truck bill is gonna bleed you dry!"

He laughed at his joke and Max walked around the rear bumper and stopped next to the driver's side door.

"Go on," Dewey said, motioning with his arm. "Get on up in there! You didn't come this far just to lay up!"

"Really?"

"Yeah! How are you gonna operate the deal if you're not in the driver's seat?"

The truck was even more impressive up close. It had four wheels across the rear axle beam and, across the front, two wheels like a normal car. Max had to step up onto a foot rail just to reach the door handle, which was hot to the touch.

The cab smelled of coffee, French fries and cigarettes. There was paperwork strewn across the dash, and a single orange cone in the backseat.

Dewey reached into his shirt pocket and pulled out a pack of cigarettes. "That toggle there, lower-left of the steering wheel, is what we call the *stinger extender*, like a bee; get that under the tires, the switch next to it works the hydraulic lift."

Max gaped at the dashboard.

Dewey stood next to the truck and turned his head as he exhaled a huge plume of smoke. "Go ahead, you can touch 'em! You aren't gonna break the thing!"

Mr. Shippen was out in his driveway, and he rolled an empty green garbage bin into his garage. Max watched the electric garage door curl to a close behind him.

"G'head!" Dewey said again. "What're you waiting for?"

Max toggled. And as he looked over his shoulder at the tow truck bucking and shimmying to his whims, he felt something all too rare. He felt powerful.

"Hey, there!"

Max looked out the open driver's side window at Gabe, who had made his way outside, his hair poking up in all directions.

"Hey, Gabe," Max said to his brother, who had sidled up to Dewey and gazed up at the tall man.

"Gabe," Dewey said, extending his arm. Gabe stiffened and looked at him with eyes wide, then took a step back. After a few beats Dewey got the hint and took his arm down.

Sadie was at the front door again. She had a textbook under her arm, the spine open.

"You're not supposed to be out here," she said, meaning Gabe. She had to be a good 20 yards away but her voice carried fine down the front walk and out to the curb.

Gabe said nothing. (He never did.)

"I think we have to go," Max said, climbing down out of the cab.

He shut the door and Dewey dropped his cigarette into the street and stomped it out. He pulled his wallet out of his pants, slid out a card. "You ever find yourself in need of something to bring to show-and-tell at school, something like an awesome set of wheels"—he handed the card to Max—"well now, you let me know."

Max looked down at the card, the number that began with 541.

Dewey climbed into the cab. "And don't play with fire," he said with a wink before firing up the engine and driving away.

***

Max explained away the smoky smell in his room as the remnants of the summer fire season. Neither he nor Sadie had told their parents about the flaming science assignment, for which Max managed to get an extension from his teacher. He hid the rather large burn mark on his desk with a rather large new desk blotter, which had set him back $8.99 at Office Max, and, as promised, Dewey bought him a new binder.

It was a mixed blessing that Max and Sadie could get away with pretty much anything—on the plus side they could get away with pretty much anything, but on the minus side that was because their parents paid more attention to 10-year-old Gabe.

This year, for example, their mother had decided fifth grade was agreeing with Gabe because he seemed to be making more eye contact. She and Max's dad were obsessed with Gabe's eye contact and his "sensory diet," which Max knew had nothing to do with food but was "a detailed activity plan" to give Gabe the best chance to someday "get focused and organized like you and your sister." (Their father's words.) Maybe someday he'd even go to Bridge, like Max and Sadie. Max hoped so.

CHAPTER

Max had been hanging out with Dewey for nearly three weeks, during which time Dewey had spent about 21 days saying they were on a hot streak. What he really meant was he, Dewey, was on a hot streak on the video poker machine—*Aces High!*—in the lobby of the Red Lion down by the Boise River. Max was pretty sure his bike could ride there without him by now.

Dewey was a gambler, and a pretty seasoned one by the look of it. He was always calm, pulling up to the machines like he was simply punching a time card, pressing the buttons like he was working on an assembly line. He said if only Max lived in Las Vegas they could make some real money, and fast. He said, more than once, that this better be their secret and not to tell his mom and dad, and to "use discretion" regarding his siblings.

"So tell me again why I can't mention you're in town?" Max asked.

"The gambling," Dewey said. "The gambling—your mother wouldn't approve."

They hit machines in other hotels, too, "in order to keep the Man off our backs," Dewey said. He never really explained who "the Man" was, but Max kind of figured it out; he took "the Man" to mean "authority."

"Now we're getting somewhere," Dewey said every time *Aces High!* paid off.

"Am I lucky?" Max asked.

"You're lucky," Dewey said.

"What do you mean I'm lucky?"

❀ ❀ ❀

The first time Max asked about luck, and how in the world Dewey had gotten it in his head that Max was some sort of lucky rabbit's foot, was a little more than three weeks earlier. They were on the phone, Max having used Dewey's business card to phone him to arrange a time to bring the truck to Bridge Academy for show and tell.

"You know, lucky," Dewey said on the phone. "Like the shirt says: L-U-C-K-Y."

"Who says?" Max asked, remembering he'd owned just such a sweatshirt. It said *LUCKY* right on the front. It was a brand of clothing, though, not an adjective.

"I says," Dewey said.

"Why?"

"I don't know." Dewey sighed into the phone, exasperated. "Why does guacamole turn brown when you put it in the refrigerator? I've just got a feeling, that's all."

Max scrunched up his face. "Well, okay, if you say so. Just get to the school like five minutes early. Mr. Purdue is a stickler about getting started on time."

He had felt proud to bring Uncle Dewey to auto shop. Dewey had a totally awesome truck, and the kids liked him. Still, Max hesitated when Dewey slipped him a note just before he left: "Meet me at the Red Lion after school. It's down by the river. It's nothing weird. We won't even leave the lobby. Let's see how lucky you are."

The bell rang at 3:10, and Max got on his bike. Dewey was waiting in the air-conditioned lobby with its chintzy fake-wood couch and chairs. The air was stale and the velour couch cushions—burgundy and forest green—were bald on the heavily trafficked high spots.

A skinny guy with nerdy, black, plastic-framed eyeglasses manned the registration desk clear across the room from the video poker machine, but he paid them no mind. Max pulled up a chair next to Dewey, who was sipping from a straw stuck into a Styrofoam cup of soda with lots of ice. He was slipping quarters into the slot.

"That's it," Dewey said. "You just sit there and radiate luck and provide Uncle Dewey some moral support. And don't worry. You'll get your share. No one works for free."

Max adjusted the set of brass knuckles in the breast pocket of his shirt. His best friend Andy said if he was going to do this, then he should at least bring a set of brass knuckles in case Uncle Dewey turned out to be some sort of nut job.

"Here, blow on this." Dewey handed Max a quarter; Max blew on it.

Sure enough, the machine bleeped and blinked as Dewey sat back and smiled, clasping his enormous hands together. "Now we're getting somewhere!"

Could it really be that simple? Max blowing on a quarter and inserting it into a machine for it to multiply into several quarters?

Max got to his feet so he could see how many credits were now on the machine: 40. If that was 40 quarters worth of credits, Dewey had just won a quick and easy 10 bucks.

A few guests trickled through the lobby, but none of them paid Max and Dewey much notice. Dewey wore cutoff jeans and a white t-shirt and those dirty Converse sneakers. Max wore what he'd worn to school: short-sleeved collared shirt, sage green, and a pair of tan slacks.

"C'mon, we've got to get going," Dewey said after winning what he later said was just over seventy dollars at *Aces High!*

Get going? To Max's mind, he may as well have suggested they light the place on fire. "What do you mean? You're on a roll! Keep going!"

"Kid," Dewey said, "you'll learn that this is a marathon, not a sprint."

Max looked across the room at the hotel's registration desk, then back at the blinking lights of the video poker machine. "What's running got to do with it?"

"We quit now, we can come back again," Dewey said.

"And if we don't?"

"If we don't," Dewey said, nodding to the man behind the registration desk, "then we get our butts thrown out of here."

Dewey handed Max a twenty-dollar bill. "Call me and we'll do it again."

Then he disappeared down the hall, bound for his room, Max assumed.

Their second meeting would be just like the first, and the third and fourth and every meeting after that wouldn't change much, either.

Was Max lucky? Maybe. He didn't know. It was fun to think so as he worked the pedals, breezing past the joggers and dog walkers as he biked the greenbelt home, his pockets full. That was how it went day after day, Dewey winning, Max feeling as if he was getting away with something. They met at other hotels, too, to hit other machines, each with its own corny, card-lingo name followed by the obligatory exclamation point.

Full House!

Royal Flush!

Gold Rush!

"How much have you made?" Sadie asked toward the end of the third week.

"About eighty dollars," Max said. (The first day had been an aberration; Dewey had given Max extra.)

"I'm going to need a percentage of that," Sadie said.

"For what?"

"Hush money," she said.

"Five percent," Max said.

"Twenty."

"Ten," Max said.

"Deal."

There weren't any casinos in Boise, but there were 16 hotels with video poker machines—and three bowling alleys. Dewey won at all of them, and used some of his earnings to purchase a pair of yellow-and-black mountaineering boots, which went halfway up his shins.

Watching a person play video poker was dull, but Max was making more than Andy got for his paper route, and had even improved his grades. He studied while Dewey played.

One day the tow truck simply went away. Dewey finally had to surrender it to a "collection agency," he explained, when Sonny threatened "legal action." In the last week, Dewey had started driving a "decommissioned police cruiser" (his words), which he bought with some of his poker winnings. "It's an old Crown

Vic," Dewey said. Max bluffed a knowing nod.

But driving around in an old police cruiser was fun, too. Max imagined himself as a lawman on patrol for mischief in the streets of Boise, and Dewey laughed at all the other cars that slowed down in front of them. "They think I'm a cop!" he said.

Max laughed. It really was kind of funny.

❈ ❈ ❈

Sadie agreed to join her mother and Gabe on their trip to the mall for one reason and one reason only. But as the three of them strode through Dillard's and bypassed Auntie Annie's pretzels and American Outfitters and smelled the fresh-baked cookies at Mrs. Fields, Sadie began to realize she had made a stupid strategic error.

It wasn't that she didn't have the money—now that she was getting a small kick-back from Max she could afford some of the finer things her peers were talking about wearing, garments they told Sadie drove the boys wild. But how on earth was she supposed to just duck into Victoria's Secret, grab some enticing underthings, pay, hide the distinctive pink and white bag, and rejoin her family without her mother noticing?

There was no way she was about to tell her mom, whose reaction Sadie could already hear in her head: "Age inappropriate," her mom would say, if not worse.

But was there a minimum age for lingerie? Sadie didn't think so, and she was fairly certain Graham Godwin wouldn't think so, either. She was fairly certain he would be thrilled at her purchase, if they ever got that far.

What *was* age inappropriate was that Sadie, Gabe and their mom were now walking into the Boise Town Square Mall Build-A-Bear, with all of its smiling creatures stuffed with non-toxic fluff and adorned with plastic eyes and button noses that absolutely would not fall off and fatally gag some hungry toddler.

With her mother and brother in tow, Sadie had sort of hoped she wouldn't run into anyone from school, but Build-A-Bear? Now she was kicking herself for not wearing a disguise.

"Mom, Gabe's 10. Don't you think he's a little old for this?"

"Hon, I'm just following doctor's orders. Cynthia says he needs a friend, someone to practice talking to who won't judge him. We'll need to name him. The bear, I mean. He'll have to have a name."

"Or she," Sadie said.

"Right," her mom said. "Or she."

They looked down at Gabe, who had picked out not a teddy bear but a pink monkey with a silver bow and a tiny tuft of pink "hair" atop her head, rising straight up like a pink flame. The monkey had jug ears, purple eyes, and no discernable nose but two nostrils.

Their mother guided Gabe to the "filling station," where he took some convincing to relinquish his grip on the monkey. Some oily-faced kid blew a bunch of fluff into a hole in the monkey's back. Gabe dressed the thing in a white t-shirt and a plaid skirt, and some white-and-pink tennis shoes—he also insisted on a pair of white and pink roller skates for later—and they were done.

As they walked out of the mall they went right past Victoria's Secret, Sadie's mother oblivious as both Sadie and, yes, Gabe, too, gaped at the racy, flesh-colored window dressing.

Evidently he liked pink. Sadie sighed. This had been a terrible mistake. Graham Godwin was going to be gravely disappointed, if they got that far.

CHAPTER

Word had gotten out about Max's tall friend with the cool tow truck, and then the cool police cruiser, and Max felt their friendship, if that was what it was, afforded him more social cachet than he previously enjoyed at Bridge Academy (which was no social cachet at all).

Without Dewey, Max was just Max, the pear-shaped kid with the freckles and the goggle glasses, but with Dewey there was a whiff of excitement about him, danger even, and this, Max decided, was worth whatever risk he might be taking. And it was potentially somehow, he didn't know how, going to make him, Max Buras, more interesting than a soup stain to Susannah Jurevicious.

As anyone in the Intermountain Independent Schools Athletic Association knew, Susannah Jurevicious played volleyball, which, Max had noticed even with his poor eyesight, meant she spent a good deal of time wearing skimpy, tight shorts. Only she didn't just play volleyball, she led the league in kills among all ninth grade girls.

Susannah Jurevicious was also three or four inches taller than Max, but he reasoned that this was because she was a year ahead of him in school. Hadn't both his mother and Dr. Steve said he just hadn't "hit his growth spurt yet," and what did height matter, anyway? She could be a verifiable giantess, and it still wouldn't change the fact that her lustrous, flaxen hair made Max's chest feel funny and his temperature rise. She had *womanly curves*, although Max tried not to think of her that way as it skeeved him out to think of Susannah in the terms his grandmother used to describe his sister.

Max did not play sports. Although he'd been intrigued to find he wore the same eyewear as many of the 1980s-era Los Angeles Lakers—Andy had shown him a library book attesting to this fact—and Andy had bought him a Los Angeles Lakers jersey, Max was too short to be any good at basketball. He couldn't play baseball, either, as his poor eyesight left him unable to track anything moving quite so fast as a pitch.

No, the closest Max came to anything remotely athletic was his unpaid job as manager of the Bridge Academy golf team. He cleaned clubs and shoes, secured tee times, bought the golf balls from the local sporting goods store and handed them out, washed the brown van that brought them all to and from the course. He never played.

It was a strange job, but it fulfilled his PE credit.

Dewey had used a golf term upon their first meeting: *You didn't come this far to lay up.* It meant, *sometimes you've just got to go for it,* or something like that. How he knew Max would have any idea what he was talking about, or whether he knew, Max had no idea. But he did, in fact, know what Dewey meant. Max spoke golf.

The job as manager of the Bridge golf team afforded Max an in, sort of, with the cool crowd that otherwise would have been unavailable to him. For example, he might have found out that Peter Whiting, Bridge's No. 1 golfer, was dating Susannah Jurevicious, but he never would have learned the color of her bra (white).

Max was glad he knew, just because, but somehow this knowledge made him feel a little guilty.

❈ ❈ ❈

In the middle of the team's fall season, life began to get complicated because that's when either his mom or his dad—he never did find out which one—found a mostly empty pack of Pall Mall cigarettes under one of the couch cushions in their living room—Dewey Tomlinson's Pall Mall cigarettes.

"Max Buras," his father said, catching Max mid-chew over a packet of graham crackers in the kitchen. "I need you to come out here right now."

His mother was holding up the cigarettes with her thumb and forefinger, as if it was a pair of soiled underpants. "Honey, do you know anything about this?"

Max felt his eyes dancing around his head in the same way Dewey's eyes had darted around in his head when he was on the lookout for Sonny of Sonny's Towing.

"Uh," Max said, trying valiantly to work up some saliva in his mouth.

"Honey," his mother repeated.

Boy, where was a glass of water when you really needed one?

"No," Max said finally. "No, I don't."

His father turned his head toward the hallway, and the bedrooms. "Sadie!"

Uh, oh.

Max's sister came padding out of her room in a new looking pair of knock-off Uggs and pink and white Hello Kitty pajamas. Her hair was mussed, and she looked up at their mother and realized what this was all about and smiled at Max.

"You've got to be kidding me," Sadie said. "You think those are mine?"

Max was pretty sure they didn't think any such thing. He was pretty sure they'd decided if they were going to accuse Max, they'd better accuse his older sister, too, lest they appear to be playing favorites. Of course they did favor her, and why not? She was better looking, she was smarter, and she was infinitely more popular than Max could ever be.

She was also a pill. At least she'd done their parents the courtesy of removing her giant pink headphones, which she now held in her hands in front of her. She gave Max a knowing smirk, and he beseeched her with his eyes not to squeal.

"Andy," Max blurted, surprising even himself.

His father stopped cold. "I beg your pardon?"

"They're Andy's," Max repeated.

Sadie snorted a laugh and Max shot her a nasty look, although he suspected it would get lost in translation, what with his thick goggle glasses and their stupid stretchy headband.

"They're Andy's?" their mother asked, as if that might help her digest this foul piece of news. She disappeared into the kitchen with the cigarettes and Max heard the lid of the garbage open and close.

His father held his gaze. "If he ever tries to offer…"

"Don't worry, Dad," Max said as Sadie headed off back down the hall toward her room. "He's already said he's quitting."

This seemed to mollify his father, who leaned back off the balls of his feet.

"He might go out for track," Max added, surprising himself again.

His father brightened. "Is that right? Good for him. What event?"

What event? Good grief. He should have quit while he was ahead.

"Hammer toe," Max said, but that didn't sound right even as the words spilled out of his mouth.

His dad frowned, as if trying to remember whether he'd replaced the gas cap on the Subaru. "Hammer *throw*?"

"Right," Max said. "That one. Yep. That's the event."

His father looked unconvinced. "You sure they're not yours?"

"Not mine," Max said, offering his most disarming smile.

"Huh," his dad said. "I don't believe you for a second, but feel free to tell me the truth when you feel up to it." Then he walked away.

Max tried to will his heart to stop lurching around in his ribcage. He knew he was never going to hear the end of this from Sadie, whose smile had seemed to suggest she found the whole episode amusing. Or maybe she'd been smirking at the prospect of additional hush money from her suddenly wealthy little brother.

❈ ❈ ❈

"You smoke," Max told Andy at school the next day.

"I what?"

"I'm afraid you smoke," Max said again. It was just the two of them at their usual humongous, way too big table. Sadie was across the room, among friends, their table's every square inch of white plastic obscured by the popular and the pretty.

"My parents found Uncle Dewey's cigarettes," Max said. "In the couch. He comes to my house once and he leaves his stupid cigarettes in the cushions. You smoke. Can you just say you smoke? If they ask?"

"Yeah, right," Andy said. "My mom won't even let me eat gluten. You told them I smoke?"

"No!" Max said. "Well, yes."

Max watched Susannah Jurevicious walk across the room with her lunch tray.

"Geez, thanks a lot," Andy said. "Why can't you just tell them Dewey smokes? Is he supposed to be quitting? Is he Mormon? He have lung cancer or something?"

Susannah put her tray on the little conveyor belt that went back to the kitchen and turned to walk toward the exit, and Max realized his best friend was looking at him expectantly. "What?"

"Never mind," Andy said.

"Sorry," Max said, refocusing. "About the cigarettes, I mean—I panicked."

"Yeah, you did. You owe me big time."

And that was how Max's only friend became not just Andy Hastings, but Andy Hastings who was courageously trying to quit smoking.

CHAPTER

For some reason Max could only guess about, Gabe now seemed to be carrying a pink monkey around with him everywhere he went; *Georgia*, he called it, or rather he'd written it on the monkey's shirt. This was only one of the reasons why at church, in Religious Exploration class, Max prayed for his weird, broken brother, who lived in a silent prison in his head.

There wasn't very much traditional praying in this church, since it was Unitarian Universalist and not very God-centered most of the time. Religious Ed class was mostly about activities and sometimes a snack, but not so much asking "Him" for help. Max prayed anyway.

He probably wouldn't have even known how to pray, were it not for watching people do it on TV, but he took some time to himself while R.E. teacher, Elton, had one of the kids light the pretend chalice and everyone else mumbled the words on the sign about how this was the church of the loving heart and the helping hands and so on and so forth. Max could never get the hand movements right as he recited the oath—he would be terrible at sign language—so it seemed just as well that his lips and his thoughts were moving off-script as a silent prayer unspooled in his head:

Lord, known as God, source and many other names, please help my brother Gabe to come into his body and his mind and at least learn how to say his own name. Lord, he is 10 and he can't even talk, for the love of—Lord, he is 10. Amen.

For the first half of the lesson, Gabe, as ever, walked around the perimeter of the room softly humming to himself as his fingers worked the nametag that should have been hanging around his neck—alas the tag's string had come untethered at one end and the tag hung limp around his belly-button. Max wondered if he should try to fix it, but as it would only upset his brother, he decided against such an intervention.

Gabe did not like to be touched, or even the threat of being touched.

But he seemed pleased when teacher Elton made him the lead role as the kids acted out the day's story. It was about Nasrudin, who was either a penniless Mulla or a penniless Muslim or maybe both (Max was having trouble paying attention) who shows up to a dinner party in shabby clothes asking if he might join the elaborate festivities in progress.

"So here's this shabby character who shows up at the door," Elton said.

The kids draped a couple of worn handkerchiefs over Gabe's shoulders to signify Nasrudin's shabbiness. Gabe stopped and looked down at his shoulders. When he resumed walking, a puff of air caught under both kerchiefs at once and they fell to the floor. The kids laughed and Max felt a wave of shame.

"Shut up!" he should have said. "That's MY BROTHER!" But that was a better version of Max. This version just laughed along with the others, too cowardly to come to Gabe's defense. Max was as useless as the pink monkey Gabe brought with him everywhere, which now sat propped up on a table in the middle of the room.

Elton continued: "The guests let Nasrudin in but ignored him in his shabby clothing. Nasrudin leaves the party and changes into some much more expensive clothes."

The kids scurried after Gabe, who was off in the corner of the room playing with his nametag again, and draped a gold-brocaded swatch of fabric over his shoulders now to signify Nasrudin's improved outfit. Gabe looked at the swatch of fabric resting upon his shoulders; Elton looked back down at his script and continued: "Nasrudin comes back to the party and, wearing his upgraded and fancier attire, and is much more welcomed, this time with a meal. But Nasrudin picks up his bowl of food and begins to feed it to his coat!"

Again, the kids laughed as Gabe began pretending to spoon-feed the gold-brocaded swatch of fabric.

"Who can tell me what the moral of this story is?" Elton asked.

"Don't discriminate," Jaden Smith said, with her best cutesy smile.

"Yeah," Jethro said. "Don't be a tool. That's the moral."

"Right," Elton said. "Well, I mean, something like that—a little more like what Jaden said, no offense, Jethro. And why do you think Nasrudin feeds his coat?"

Someone had passed gas and Max heard a rising swell of tittering.

"Aw, Gabe!" Jethro said.

Now they were really laughing. Gabe looked up, confused.

"Knock it off!" Max shouted. The laughter stopped.

"Please be respectful." Elton's eyes registered surprise at Max's strident defense of his brother, or maybe he was worried for his job. This was supposed to be a tolerant church, and here they were blaming Gabe for a silent but deadly one, treating Gabe, who couldn't even form the words to defend himself, like he was the family dog.

"Why do you think—" Elton started, but Max had had enough.

"Because he realizes the people at the party welcomed only what he was wearing," Max said, keeping his eyes on the accused Gabe, who had shed his startled look and was back in Gabe Land, wandering around the room, humming non-musically to himself. "They didn't welcome the man underneath the clothing."

"Good!" Elton said. "I see you read the lesson."

Max looked at his watch. They had another 15 minutes before their parents were to come get them. No one spoke.

"Drawing time!" Elton said. "I don't think we have a snack."

He hurried over to the cupboard in the corner of the room and hastily gathered a roll of butcher-block paper, which he tore into large swaths. He taped these to the table, and set out the markers and crayons and colored pencils in three recycled tin cans absent their labels.

They drew.

❈ ❈ ❈

Inevitably, Gabe took up more than a third of their parents' attention, but neither Max nor Sadie complained. They knew they were the lucky ones. *Social anxiety disorder and inattentive ADHD*, said one doctor. *Selective mutism*, said another. No, no, said a third, it was much more serious than that; it was *Asperger syndrome* or full-blown *autism.*

Max had heard him talk, but it had been a while—about four years. That's how long it had been since the two were out on the front lawn having a catch when they'd watched Mr. Shippen's Yorkshire Terrier run into the street. Max always wondered if Gabe had somehow been struck dumb by the sight and sound of it, the screeching rubber, an awful thud and a high-pitched yelp as the air left that furry, four-legged, black and tan body.

Multiple speech therapists, a restricted diet, special schools, a guy who came over to the house to play the bowl and meditate for five and a half days— they'd tried everything to get him out of the quiet, dark place inside his head. The built-in bookshelf in their living room was filled with tomes on various disorders and traditional and nontraditional therapies, but nothing worked. He was a stump- er, "an enigma," Max's dad said. "Misunderstood," his mom said. But Max loved his brother just the same, or maybe even more.

Gabe did not go to Bridge, but instead attended Circle of Friends, which Max had never really liked. He was pretty sure Gabe was smart enough go to Bridge, if they just gave him a chance. No, he didn't say much, but he knew what was what. He was all but unbeatable at concentration, the card game. It was al- most like he could see through the backs of the cards.

"Circle," as they called it, was basically a group of about 18 people meeting in the basement of St. Michael's, the church right across the street from the state capitol building. Among the adults there were two special education teachers, a social worker, a home health aid, and the rest were parent volunteers— Max's mom spent a bit of time there. Then there were the kids, almost all of them needing quite a lot of extra help, more even than Gabe.

Max thought Gabe didn't fit in at CF. It wasn't like he wasn't smart. He was excellent in geometry, and pretty good in math in general. He could read, his written book reports signaling that he'd understood what he'd read. And although Max and Sadie hadn't heard him talk in a long time, he definitely could talk—he'd done it twice in the last year, both times apparently surprising himself with the sound of his voice. The first time had been at home and their mother had heard him; upon plunging into a warm bath Gabe had sighed and said, "Otter," and then looked around like he'd heard a ghost. They now believed that this had been a mash-up "ah" and "water." The second time he'd been at school. According to both teachers and the home health aid the class had been watching a silent movie and, during an especially funny scene, Gabe, howling with laughter, finally caught up to his breath and said, "Mr. Bean!"

In both cases efforts to get him to repeat himself had failed.

❦ ❦ ❦

In church, after they had all acted out the *Nasrudin* tale, Gabe pulled up from his slow-motion tour of the perimeter of the room and grabbed a seat at the table, the first of them to sit down, ready as ever to draw parallelograms. Max took the seat to his brother's right, and contemplated the blank piece of paper in front of him. He wondered when his brother would emerge from whatever type of developmental fog this was; Cynthia and Dr. Steve had said it could be any day, or it could also be never, and they just had to wait him out.

Religious education teacher Elton found some Goldfish crackers in the cupboard and filled a half a dozen small Dixie cups with them before triumphantly setting them before the kids. "I lied! We do have a snack!" He filled up some cups of water. "That looks great, Gabe!"

Max made no move for the pens or crayons or pencils, content to watch Gabe draw. He really could draw a good parallelogram. Max briefly considered drawing Dewey, standing in front of *Aces High!* He was a little strange looking and he didn't smell great—the cigarettes. And what did he mean by calling himself "the black sheep" of the family?

At least he no longer came over to the house—he'd only come over twice, once out of the blue when Max's science homework caught fire, and a second time when it was raining and Max didn't feel much like biking to the ancient hotel and asked to be picked up.

Max wondered if he was really as lucky as Dewey said. Sure, the guy kept winning at video poker, but was that really proof of anything? Maybe the machine was broken. No, Max wanted some "unassailable proof," a term he'd heard on one of the law shows his parents watched.

He didn't have to wait very long.

❈ ❈ ❈

Sadie finally made it back to the mall, this time with Missy McGrath, who was already driving. They skipped Build-A-Bear and went straight to Victoria's Secret.

With the money she'd earned by keeping her mouth shut about her brother and "Uncle Dewey," Sadie bought the fanciest underwear she'd ever owned: it was turquoise and soft and gave off a cool shine and the bottom part of the two-piece set was cut in a way she knew her mother wouldn't approve of at all. Graham Godwin was going to love it.

Missy bought some kind of black one-piece that was far sexier than anything Sadie had ever imagined herself wearing, and her heart raced and her stomach did the Macarena as they walked out of the store.

"Well, hey there!"

Sadie stopped and looked up at Dewey Tomlinson, who was by himself, in a pair of cutoff shorts, a button-down, short-sleeved, yellow shirt, and what appeared to be a new pair of hiking boots. He held the remnants of a cinnamon-covered pretzel, about half eaten.

"Oh, hi—Dewey."

"Sadie," he said. He looked over at Missy. "And ..."

"This is Missy," Sadie said.

"Hi," Missy said. They did not shake hands.

For the second time in her latest trips to the mall, Sadie kicked herself for not wearing a disguise. And now—oh, geez, now Dewey had his head down; he was gaping at their Victoria's Secret bags. He looked back at the store, its pink and flesh-colored windows plastered with large photos of scantily clad models.

"How old are you?" he asked, looking at Sadie.

"Fifteen," Missy said.

"Not you," Dewey said. "Your friend here."

"Fifteen," Sadie said.

"Huh," Dewey said.

"He's my uncle, or something," Sadie said to Missy, who looked confused.

"Oh," Missy said.

"Well, we'd better get going," Sadie said hopefully.

"Missy," Dewey said, pulling out a tattered leather wallet. He fished a bill out of the billfold. "Do me a favor, yeah? Get me a small coffee, no cream?"

He nodded at the Starbucks above them, on the mall's second level. "And get yourself something, too."

"Okay!" Missy said, before skipping off toward the stairs.

"Hang on," Dewey said. "Sadie, you want anything?"

"Um, no, thanks," Sadie said. This was all getting a little weird.

"Back in a flash!" Missy turned and skipped up the stairs.

"You have a little arrangement with your brother," Dewey said.

"An arrangement?" Sadie said, but she knew she was cooked. Evidently Max had told Dewey about the hush money she'd demanded—money that had paid for the turquoise lingerie she'd just bought.

"You want me to spell it out for you?" Dewey said.

"No," Sadie said, looking up at the Starbucks, where Missy was at the end of a short line.

"Good!" Dewey said. "Because that little arrangement stops now. The money part stops, that is; the hush part will continue, on both of our parts. I'll be as quiet as church mouse." He nodded at her Victoria's Secret bag. "Just as long as you are. Just don't go and get yourself pregnant and make me regret not telling your mother you're buying $30 underwear."

Sadie looked down at her sandals and wondered whether she should mention her underwear had cost $50.

"Uh, no," she said. "I mean, I won't. But I wasn't planning on doing that, anyway. And what do you care?"

"I'm your Uncle Dewey! Of course I care!"

Neither of them spoke for a good 10 seconds.

"It's a free country," Sadie finally said. That sounded good.

"Sure is," Dewey said. "We're all free to make as many bad choices as we want."

Again they stood sizing each other up as an awkward silence fell over them.

Missy pulled up with a coffee in each hand, and gave the smaller one to Dewey.

"Thanks for the joe!" he said. "You can keep the change. So delightful to meet you, Missy." He took a tiny sip. "Mmmm, that's good coffee. Make good choices, girls! Good choices!"

With that, he gave a funny little salute with his free hand and walked away.

CHAPTER

Max Buras, to the principal's office.

Max looked up at the loudspeaker mounted in the upper-right corner of his fifth-period Spanish class. It was Monday, and a cold rain fell outside.

A familiar, prickly heat crept up Max's neck as 23 heads swiveled to gawk at him. One of these was the gorgeous head of Susannah Jurevicious, who sat in front of him and whose lustrous, flaxen hair smelled of honeysuckle, occasionally transporting Max to another place and time—usually involving a tropical island, ukulele music, and drinks with pineapple wedges.

"Me?" Max mouthed to the teacher, his index finger pointing at his chest.

Mr. Raymundo nodded toward the door. Max got up, his heart pounding. He lifted his backpack off the back of his chair and tried to force a smile, like he frequently got called to the principal's office, that was just how he rolled, and everything was "all good."

All *was* good until he heard a percussive *thwack* behind him and realized he'd forgotten to zip his backpack closed, allowing his leaden math textbook to fall out and land on the floor just a few paces from the door. A few kids laughed. Max felt his cheeks redden.

"Silencio," Mr. Raymundo said as Max picked up his book and hurried out of the classroom.

His thoughts formed a meteor shower that raged in his skull as he walked down the mostly empty hallway festooned with posters for the upcoming Halloween dance, costume contest, and varsity football game. On the one hand, he'd never been to the principal's office, so this was an exciting "voyage of discovery," as the voiceover might say if his life were a movie trailer. On the other hand, this was a movie his parents weren't going to like.

The principal's office was in the corner of the building, and overlooked the street and the official student "drop-off zone." (No idling engines, please.)

Her door was open.

"Hello, Max," Mrs. McQuaid said. "Have a seat, please."

She had arranged everything just so on her desk: Pink, flowery box of Kleenex; silver picture frames that Max could only see the backs of; a tiny gold trophy of some kind; a navy blue and white Bridge Academy mug full of pencils, each sharpened to a murderous point.

Mrs. McQuaid, someone told him once, was really a softy at heart. Someone else had said she was a power-mad tyrant.

"I think you and I both know why you're here," she said.

Max wondered if this was some sort of trick question, and if a power-mad tyrant could smell like a bouquet of lilacs, like the perfume samples in his mom's magazines. "Uh," he stammered. "We do?"

Mrs. McQuaid leaned back in her chair, strummed the desk with her fingers. "Mrs. Hickenlooper? Third-period math? The M&M's? Ring a bell?"

Oh, no. Max felt his hot cheeks. He never should have asked the universe for "unassailable proof" of his luckiness. He knew immediately what had happened.

Mrs. Hickenlooper had put a jar of M&M's on her desk—718 M&M's, in fact, if Max remembered correctly. Suddenly Max knew exactly why he was here. His ears were on fire, his head was ringing, and the back of his throat inexplicably tasted like metal.

"Did someone steal them?" he asked.

If only Andy were here, Max thought, he could've testified to Max's preference for Junior Mints.

"In a manner of speaking," Mrs. McQuaid said. She pushed back from her desk, got to her feet and began to work her hands into a chapel as she paced in front of the window that looked out onto the front lawn and the school's designated and highly regulated student drop-off zone.

"In a manner of speaking…" She stopped pacing, dropped her hands down to her sides and, unsmiling, looked down at him squirming in his seat. "In a manner of speaking, you did."

"I did?" Max said.

"Oh, not literally," Mrs. McQuaid said, pulling her chair out and sitting again. "The jar is still on her desk, or I can only assume it is."

She steepled her hands again and looked across the desk at Max. He tried to hold her gaze. "So what happened? Why am I here? What's the…"

She cut him off. "Max, did you count the M&M's?"

"No!"

He wondered how she envisioned him doing this, perhaps sneaking into school after hours and dumping the whole jar out on a pile of spread out newspapers.

"No," he said again. "I didn't count them. Are you saying I had the winning guess?"

"Oh, you did indeed—right on the number!" Mrs. McQuaid laughed.

Max laughed, too, but regretted it. He wondered if he should pretend to be excited, but that didn't seem like a good idea, either. "This is impossible," he said.

Mrs. McQuaid smiled. "Impossible?"

"I never win anything!" Max blurted, as if that could save him now.

"So you just guessed the exact number of M&M's," she said, squinting at him. "All seven hundred and eighteen M&M's—you guessed that, out of thin air."

"I guess so," Max said, but he immediately regretted it. I *guess* so. I *guess* so. Gawd. Now she was going to think he was making fun of her.

"I find that very hard to believe," she said, getting to her feet again. She took off her glasses and rubbed her eyes with a thumb and forefinger, then looked out the window at the drop-off area. "Remind me to bring you with me next time I go to Jackpot."

Jackpot, Max knew, was a town in Nevada where adults sometimes went to gamble. It was where Christopher Mobius, who really did smoke, had watched his father "go bust" and then go to jail, according to the eighth grade rumor mill.

So that was it, then. He'd been too perfect. Max wondered if he could look at his watch without seeming rude, as he didn't want to be late for auto shop, but Mrs. McQuaid spun around to face him again. "May I remind you this is a math exercise, Max? Or at least it was supposed to be. Did you even think to measure the diameter of the jar?"

Max tried to remember which one was diameter. "No."

"And the radius?"

He felt the shame begin to well up in his throat. "No."

"The height?"

"No."

"Then how did you arrive at such an informed decision? Please, do tell." She put her glasses back on and sat down again.

Mrs. McQuaid, Max decided, got up and sat down and waved her hands around in the air even more than the actors on the law shows. He also decided she looked better without the glasses.

He weighed his options. If he told her he'd had a sneaking suspicion that this might happen with the M&M's, she'd think he was crazy. And if he told her about Dewey Tomlinson, there was no telling what she might do.

"I don't know," he finally said. "Lucky guess?"

She smiled, shook her head, looked down at something on her desk, and back up.

"You've never been in here," she said, more of a statement than a question.

"No," Max said.

"And that's why I'm going to take you at your word," she said, getting up again. "I must be the most gullible principal in the Treasure Valley. You're free to go."

CHAPTER 7

So he was lucky. But why was he lucky now, all of a sudden, after 13 years of ordinary?

He wasn't lucky when he was born with such terrible eyesight. He wasn't lucky when he and Andy were jumping stairs on their Rollerblades and Max landed on his chin, splitting it open like an orange. He'd needed six stitches that day, and each one had really hurt.

Lucky? Why was he lucky? Why now? He heard the echo of Dewey's voice: *Why does guacamole turn brown?* "Oxygen," Max should've said. "Oxygen." He'd looked it up.

But was being lucky necessarily a good thing? Sure, Max was now in possession of a little extra spending money on account of his adventures with Dewey. But what did he need money for? He hadn't spent his share on much, so far, except for some new golf gloves and balls for the Bridge team, as the school's $600 yearly stipend didn't quite cover everything.

He was also in possession of 718 M&M's.

Word got out pretty fast that he'd guessed the exact number in the jar, and the general consensus on campus seemed to be that he'd cheated.

❄ ❄ ❄

"Nice work, Buras," Pete Whiting said.

It was a gray fall day, the day after the M&M's' fiasco, and Max was loading up the root beer-colored team van for a highly anticipated golf match against Star Christian. Bridge and Star were tied atop the conference standings.

"But I don't know if you really need to be eating that many M&M's," Whiting added, "if you catch my drift."

The guys on the team stood off to the side in their navy shorts and orange polo shirts, a couple of them in white belts, all of them a little quieter than usual, which Max attributed to nerves. He wore a pair of navy slacks and, under his gray Costco parka, an ill-fitting orange polo shirt made of some sort of synthetic "breathable" fabric, which Max felt self-conscious about since he wasn't really on the team.

Mr. Raymundo, the Bridge golf coach and Spanish teacher, waddled out the school's front door and gave the signal to hop in, grab a seat and buckle up. Round bellied, and with his ever-present push-broom mustache, Mr. R's uniform was the usual: dirty khakis and a checked flannel shirt with the sleeves rolled up just past his beefy forearms.

"That's it," Max said, sliding the door shut and shaking the van. "Let's go."

He fell into the front passenger seat as Mr. Raymundo stopped twirling the keys on his index finger and the van roared to life. As a joke, someone had taped a handwritten sign onto the dashboard that said, "THANK YOU FOR YOUR GENEROUS TIPS," above a pink, wicker basket, inside of which was a single, white dollar bill. Monopoly money.

As the van turned left and picked up speed, heading for the four-lane Interstate, Max decided Pete Whiting was his least favorite Bridge golfer. Max knew, everyone knew, the guy was going to take Susannah Jurevicious to the Halloween dance because he couldn't stop talking about it, how he was going to be Justin Timberlake from some *Saturday Night Live* skit, and Susannah was going to be someone named Elvira, Mistress of the Dark.

Max had never heard of Elvira, "Mistress of the Dark," and the previous evening—to occupy himself with something else after that day's M&M's debacle—he'd looked up this mysterious "mistress of the dark" on his father's computer. This had been an eye-opener, and upon hearing footsteps Max had had to quickly redirect his browser to an educational website about how to build model airplanes.

Max kept his hands hidden deep in the recesses of his parka as the van rumbled toward Ridgecrest Golf Course.

Most other golf teams, he knew, did not travel by van. The kids showed up on their own, usually in luxury cars driven by their parents, but Mr. Raymundo had wanted a way to foster team unity, which he called *duende*, and thus the van. What the van really led to, more than *duende*, was a bunch of kids making lewd signs to press up against the windows and trying to impress one another with supposedly true stories that Max suspected totally weren't.

In his parka pockets Max felt the weight of two-dozen new Titleist golf balls that he'd been schlepping around with him all day. He wanted them near him as much as possible, and kept cradling them with his hands, partly out of nervousness. He defended his plan thusly: What good was good luck if you didn't take it out for a spin?

The van pulled into the parking lot. It was 3:45, an overcast afternoon, about 60 degrees. From the looks of the mostly empty lot, only a few other golfers had bothered to come out to the course. Mr. Raymundo killed the engine and as the five boys behind them spilled out of the van, Max quietly unzipped a small, soft-sided cooler at his feet.

"Ammunition!" he announced as he stepped onto the blacktop.

He handed each player six balls, and for each Bridge golfer, except for one, those balls came from deep in the cozy, heated recesses of his parka pockets.

"Jesus, Buras, these golf balls are freezing," Pete Whiting said.

Using his heels, Max stuffed the soft-sided cooler under his seat, out of sight. He shrugged.

Whiting, Bridge's No. 1 golfer, looked down at his two sleeves, three balls apiece, that Max had hidden in the teachers' lounge refrigerator, behind an unreasonably large jar of mayonnaise, and brought to the course in the cooler. Whiting looked up at Max. "And why are you wearing a golf glove all the sudden? You don't even play."

The others laughed.

"Ay, silencio," Mr. Raymundo said.

"I thought I might hit a few shots on the range," Max said, flexing his gloved hand. If this was going to work, he knew he couldn't even as much as lay a finger on any of Whiting's equipment. It had to work, didn't it? If not, what was the point of his strange new superpower, or whatever it was?

Whiting looked at Max like he'd sprouted a horn.

"You're a curious case, Max Buras."

The guys meandered out onto the practice putting green and then onto the first tee, where Max held a clipboard and announced the players before they teed off. A Star Christian player gently corrected Max on the pronunciation of his name. "It's Boudroux," the kid said. "The 'X' is silent."

For the next two hours he did not endeavor to try golf. He took his glove off, set up at a table in the clubhouse, which smelled of popcorn, and tried to crack the extra credit problem in math, since whatever goodwill he'd built up with Mrs. Hickenlooper had now been obliterated amid an avalanche of M&M's. Max made his way to the concession lady and paid for a box of Junior Mints. It was a little lonely, what with everyone out playing. It always was. But as ever he told himself he could get more work done this way.

Upon their return to the clubhouse the Bridge Academy golfers were abuzz with excitement, and their scores told the story:

Alex Fisk 37; Hadley Jackson 37; Don Kennerly 38; Phil Hendrickson 39; Pete Whiting 40. Since only the best four scores counted in any given match, Whiting's 40 was rendered moot. Max grinned. "Best team score this season!" he said.

"Forget the season," Mr. Raymundo said, his cheeks ruddy from having played nine holes himself, as usual. "That's the best we've ever done in any season!"

With a score of 151, Bridge had beaten Star by a half-dozen shots.

"I made *everything* on the greens," Hadley said.

"Me, too!" Donnie added.

"Unbelievable day," Phil gushed.

The van ride back to school was abuzz with such chatter, great shots praised, superb bounces recounted, the future brighter for almost all of them.

"I don't get it," Whiting said. "I couldn't seem to buy a break today."

Max looked at his feet and ate a Junior Mint.

CHAPTER

Max had a stomachache as they rode back to school. What did he have against Whiting, anyway? And was helping only the other four guys on the team with his "golden mojo," or whatever it was that now seemed to be radiating from Max's fingertips, really going to help him get anywhere with Susannah Jurevicious?

It seemed unlikely. His stomach squawked. Maybe he'd just eaten too many Junior Mints.

He looked down at the single dollar bill in the pink wicker basket as every player but Pete went over his round shot by shot to anyone who would listen. The van pulled up to the front of the school and everyone piled out onto the curb. Max climbed into the back of the van and carefully handed everyone down his clubs. Whiting was the only one who didn't say thanks.

"We're trending up, boys," Mr. Raymundo said as four of the five boys on the team ducked into a Mercedes, two Volvos and a Mini Cooper, which only fit Phil Hendrickson's clubs if the back seats were folded down. "This could be a season to remember!"

The moms and dads pulled away from the school leaving only Whiting, who was doing his best to pretend Max and Mr. Raymundo weren't standing there waiting with him on the curb. He looked at his thick, silver-colored watch. He looked up at the darkening sky over the capitol building. He adjusted his blue and orange Bridge Golf cap, and checked his watch again.

Max decided maybe Whiting was allergic to public golf. He was a regular at Hillcrest Country Club—his dad was some kind of local real estate superstar whose photo was on a few bus benches in town. Presently, Alan Whiting drove his ridiculous car around the corner going a little too fast for a school zone and pulled to a stop next to the team van.

He didn't bother to turn his car off, and Pete went around back and threw his clubs in the back before slamming the back gate. He got in the front passenger seat and closed the door and Max watched them drive away in Alan Whiting's pearl-white Lexus SUV that seemed to have been shrink-wrapped in a gigantic American flag, along with the logo and lettering of the 2022 U.S. Open at The Country Club in Brookline, Mass., covering the front and rear side doors.

It was a truly ridiculous car—gaudy, ostentatious, pretentious. How Alan Whiting had decided that would be his son's debut U.S. Open was unclear. Pete would be around 21, Max supposed, which meant he'd be either out of college or close to it. The good news, if there was any, was that he would certainly have no doubts about what his father expected of him. Talk about pressure.

Mr. Raymundo looked down at his watch, then at Max. "My own game is as poor as ever, *amigo*—another 45 today." He shook his head. "Ay, *dios mios*. I'll see you in class. Don't forget, *amigo*, we've got a vocab quiz tomorrow, travel words—*mucho* useful!"

"Okay," Max said.

❀ ❀ ❀

"I don't get it."

Andy was sitting on the edge of his bed, legs dangling over the side, eating a cookie.

"What don't you get?" Max said.

"You think that even though you don't even play in them, you somehow control the outcome of the team's matches or tournaments or whatever they're called?"

It was times like these that Max felt grateful for the mere four-block difference between their North End houses. Instead of biking home from school, as usual, he had biked to Andy's house.

"They're called matches," Max said. "Unless there are more than two teams playing, in which case they're tournaments." He looked at the half-spent votive candle burning on Andy's desk, where Max sat. The desk also featured a

Star Trek page-a-day calendar, a corkboard and a closed Mac computer. A shallow puddle of wax had formed under the fat candle flame. Andy said his mom's cookies were giving him gas.

"So the point is," he continued, "you think you're affecting the outcome. Like you're the puppeteer?"

Max tried a bite of cookie, which was dry. He placed it back on its plate. "I guess I think I did." He tilted his head up at the scale-model arrangement of the planets hanging from the ceiling.

"How?" Andy asked.

"I guess I think I'm lucky," Max said, looking back at his best friend. It all sounded so stupid now that he was saying it aloud. "The golf balls that I touched, that I spent all day touching, went in the holes. They rocketed off trees, cart paths—however they had to, they found their targets. The guys said so. The golf balls that I went out of my way not to touch, and to actually refrigerate and bring to the course in a beer cooler, not so lucky."

Andy sighed and let his body fall backward on the bed. "Is this about your new best friend?"

"His name is Dewey. And he's not my new best friend. He's my uncle. I think. But yes, it sort of is about him. Before he told me I was lucky, I had no idea. I can barely see and I'm like four and a half feet tall and hopelessly uncoordinated and my brother—there's something wrong with him.

"But then this guy, Uncle Dewey, he shows up at our door and says I'm special, and he has me blow on his quarters, and he wins at video poker. He wins so much he won't spend more than five minutes playing any single machine because he says the hotels are gonna catch on and he's paranoid of getting kicked out. And then comes the thing with the M&M's…"

"I thought you rigged the M&M's deal," Andy interrupted.

"No!"

"All right, all right, calm down."

"I told you it was pure dumb luck," Max said. "How would I have cheated? And better yet, why would I have cheated? I don't even like peanut M&M's. I have no reason to rig it like that. Is Susannah Jurevicious going to go to the Halloween dance with me because I guessed the exact number of M&M's in the jar on Mrs. Hickenlooper's desk?"

Andy snorted out a laugh. "Yeah, right."

"That was a rhetorical question," Max said. "And then the thing with the golf balls, which I've got to be honest, really skeeved me out. I think something weird is happening here. I really do. I don't know. I might tell my parents."

Andy shot up in bed. "Good gawd, no! Get ahold of yourself!"

Max smiled despite his mood. "Okay, I won't tell my parents."

Andy sat up again in the bed. "Okay, you're on a streak," he said. "I respect that. You're on a hot streak. It's about time." He got to his feet, brushing some cookie crumbs onto the floor. "The question is, what are *we* gonna do about it?"

CHAPTER

"I spoke to Francis today," Max's mom said at dinner.

"Huh," Max said.

"Please don't use your napkin for that," his mother said.

Max looked down and realized he was cleaning his glasses, which he stopped doing. Even without them on his face he could detect Sadie smirking at him from across the table. Or maybe he was just imagining it. Her eyesight wasn't so hot, either, but their parents had splurged on LASIK surgery for her 15th birthday.

Gabe, seated to Max's right, was eating his sweet potato nuggets, with Mars, the family dog, patrolling the "DZ" (drop zone) area around Gabe's chair.

"Big Guy," Max's father started. "We know Andy isn't trying to quit smoking. We know he never *did* smoke."

With his glasses back on his face, Max saw his mother push back a smile.

Max's friendship with Andy had been going strong since they'd knocked around together as toddlers in the same playgroup. As far as Max knew, they were the only ones who'd remained friends. Denny Fulton's family had moved to Utah. Ed Squires had moved to California to live with his dad. Missy McGrath hung out in the popular clique, a closed loop to people like Max and Andy.

In any event, the problem with a friendship that went back that far was that their mothers talked.

Max leveled his eyes across the dining room and into the kitchen, letting them rest on a sheet full of Gabe's orange and brown parallelograms on display on the refrigerator door.

"We're going to need to know the real story," his father continued. "We know Steve and Francis. We know they don't even let Andy drink soda, let alone slowly kill himself with cigarettes at 13. We're going to need to know why you keep coming home smelling like smoke, and who belongs to those cigarettes your mom found in the couch. Want to tell us?"

Max looked across the table at Sadie, who shrugged. Had she squealed? What had she told them? There was no way she'd spilled everything, telling them about the mysterious arrival of Uncle Dewey, and their gambling spree. Had she? Maybe she had! Max looked at his plate; he'd hardly touched his food.

"They're mine," he said.

Sadie's mouth hung open. Gabe kept rocking back and forth in his seat and "self-soothing" (Dr. Steve's words) with humming noises while intermittently shoveling sweet potatoes into his mouth, the sound interspersed with the jangling of Mars's collar ID tags as he happily worked his little jaws, cleaning the floor.

"They're yours," Max's mother repeated.

"Well," Max said, "not exactly. Or I guess they are, sort of. I found them at the bowling alley. I've been spending quite a bit of time bowling lately."

At least that much was true, the part about spending time in bowling alleys—they had video poker machines, too, and without the prying eyes of hotel desk clerks. Dewey was big on bowling alleys.

"Did you smoke them?"

Uh, oh. Max's father had lost his congenial tone.

Max shook his head. "I was just curious. It's so smoky in those places, bowling alleys, I guess I, I sort of wondered what all the fuss was about."

He looked over at Sadie, then at Gabe, and then finally at his mother, whose face had turned to white granite, and his father, whose face was red. "I don't believe you," his father said. "Why should I believe you? Tell me why I should—"

"Harold," Max's mother said, cutting off his father before the raging inferno could gather any more momentum.

Max's forehead and ears felt hot again. He was definitely going to be grounded. Oh, well. He was getting a little too old to trick-or-treat, anyway.

CHAPTER 10

Boise wasn't a bad place to live, but Dewey had grown tired of staying at the Red Lion down by the river. Or rather, the Red Lion had tired of him.

He had been living there as well as gambling, but eventually the general manager—some guy who wore outdated glasses and a pocket protector for his button-down, short-sleeved shirts—had realized they were restocking the video poker machine with cash a lot more frequently than usual. Since the thing was right there in the lobby, clearly visible from the registration desk, it hadn't taken much detective work to deduce that Dewey—even limiting his play to five or 10 minutes at a time—was to blame.

At least they'd been polite about it when they asked him to leave.

The old Crown Vic took him to one of the highest points in the city, the Grandview Motel on Federal Way, where he rented an efficiency apartment for $205 a week. Of course the old Crown Vic may have taken him here out of habit, Dewey laughed to himself, given that it was a decommissioned police cruiser and the Grandview Motel, despite its groovy pink and blue neon sign, looked like the type of place that had seen its share of police activity.

He'd first run afoul of the law at 11, for a price-tag switcheroo at a Target in Tacoma. An older boy had put him up to it—Dewey had been too young to understand exactly what he was getting into—but he'd taken the rap. Shortly after that he'd met his first social worker. He started smoking at 13, quit school at 16, left home, and began a string of boring, low-paying jobs. It wasn't until he was in his twenties that he really screwed up.

Still, despite the Grandview's dated décor and lack of a swimming pool, and the road noise, it wasn't bad. At worst it was a lateral move from the Riverview Mobile Estates trailer park in Pendleton, but life wasn't going to get any better for him in Oregon. His future there consisted of waiting for breakdowns— these paid $200 for a hookup fee, plus the mileage surcharge for gas—which would line the pockets of Sonny and Sonny's Towing, but do little for Dewey himself, who did all the work. He'd been working for "The Man."

Plus, Dewey got lousy television reception in Pendleton. So he didn't go back.

Dewey marveled at how he'd wound up here, in a cheap efficiency apartment with a broken dresser mirror next to a busy road in southwest Idaho. He was 44 years old, and just a shade over six feet tall, 180 pounds. No wife. No kids. He could change a tire in two minutes with cars whizzing past his backside at 80 miles per hour. He could play a fairly decent game of basketball, golf, and table tennis, but he had trouble gaining weight and he could not wear a tie without extreme discomfort. He had big feet and trouble buying shoes.

His journey to Boise had been circuitous, to say the least. That day he'd first shown up at the Buras's front door, and sprung into action as a sort of volunteer firefighter, had started not at his usual stomping grounds, the Wild Horse Casino in Pendleton, Oregon, where they knew him by name, but at Cactus Pete's in Jackpot, Nevada. This had required Dewey make a six-hour drive in the tow truck, but that was a sacrifice he was willing to make for the superior amenities of Jackpot: more tables, tastier (microbrew) beers, prettier waitresses, and more golf courses.

Still, he'd lost, again—black jack, again—which was going to make it hard to pay his rent, again. Things were not going well in Pendleton, where Dewey helped people change out their flat tires or gave them a tow out on Interstate 84. Every tire, it seemed, was left rear, exactly where you didn't want it because it left you so exposed to onrushing cars. Dewey had heard this tire called "the widow-maker," and he became convinced he was going to die in the line of duty, flattened by a giant, speeding SUV while its driver jabbed at his smart phone. And for what? Sonny Simms. It was Sonny who was making the most money off of Dewey's backbreaking labor as he risked life and limb.

Who else would he really be letting down if he left Pendleton? Try as he might Dewey could think of no one save for Amarillo Slim, his name for the black and white stray cat that came around. Dewey left him (or her) bowls of Meow Mix and milk.

Sometimes, when he cursed his decisions to hit or hold, Dewey wondered if he could even beat Amarillo Slim at blackjack, (assuming, of course, Amarillo Slim had opposable thumbs and could hold the cards). Dewey was a terrible, terrible card player—it was a failing he'd proven yet again that morning in Jackpot, Nevada, just south of the Idaho border. He'd lost $230, which was all the money he'd gone there with minus $70.

Defeated and despondent, Dewey was in what the psychologists would call a suggestible state. Dewey would have called it a headache. On his way out of the casino he spied an abandoned business card lying face-up at a vacated craps table. The glossy, sharp-edged card advertised the services of *Madam Hagar: Psychic Medium for Apparitions, Poltergeists, and all things Paranormal.* There was a photo of a woman in heavy makeup and some sort of headdress, involving a lot of very complicated beadwork. She looked like Cleopatra, or Elizabeth Taylor, or Elizabeth Taylor playing Cleopatra.

"A talisman is coming your way," she told Dewey when he called the number and pressed the button indicating he agreed to be charged $14.99 a minute.

"A totem of excellent fortune," she clarified as Dewey watched some young punk with his baseball cap on backward walk up to the roulette wheel and give it a spin.

"A good luck charm," she further clarified.

The roulette wheel stopped, and the kid in the baseball cap high-fived his buddies as they erupted in a sonic boomlet of excitement that carried across the casino floor.

A good luck charm. Dewey liked the sound of that, but he got confused when he asked her to elaborate. He wanted to know what to look for, and what to do with it when he found it, but Madam Hagar only said, "Don't worry about finding it; it will find you."

He would have asked for clarification, but the call was costing him a fortune and he suddenly couldn't get out of Jackpot fast enough. The place made him feel like a loser.

As a result of his confusion, Dewey followed around a magical looking squirrel he found gathering nuts under the big tree outside a McDonald's in Twin

Falls. He'd stopped there for lunch on the long drive back to Oregon. He'd hoped to make it all the way to Boise for lunch, but his stomach had vetoed the idea.

The squirrel, black and tan with a fluffed up tail, seemed almost human-like in his economy of motion, his sense of purpose, but he scampered up the tree trunk and disappeared amid the dark canopy of leaves and branches.

Dewey went inside, sad to have parted with the squirrel but happy at the air conditioning. He bought lunch and thought he recognized a human face in his chicken nuggets, but he was too hungry, he was imagining things, he was pressing.

He was sipping on the last of his strawberry shake when he saw the kid, a boy, maybe 15 or 16 or 17, wearing a blue t-shirt that said, "LUCKY." White letters. The boy was part of a group—maybe seven or eight boys and girls—but Dewey didn't care about them. He had seen the same t-shirt on a younger boy in a Christmas card photograph stuck to the refrigerator at his mother's house in La Grande. His foster mother, actually.

"Who's he?" Dewey asked that day. "And what makes him lucky?"

His plump, white-haired foster mother, whom he'd never seen in anything other than sweatpants and a sweatshirt, told him the kid was her great nephew, her sister's grandkid. His name was Max Buras. He lived in Boise, Idaho.

A child shrieked, and Dewey, wondering if he should get some more chicken nuggets, looked out at the entanglement of bright plastic that was the Twin Falls McDonald's Playland. He let his eyes track the wailing, knee-high blond boy as he ran to his attractive blonde mother for comfort.

"Aw, Max," the woman said. "My little Maxi Max. My prince. My big, strong hero!"

Dewey's pulse jumped and he realized he was standing. He looked at the mom and her fat, little kid, and back at the teenagers, and, suddenly self-conscious, sat back down on his little metal seat. He rolled his neck and pried off the plastic lid of his cup and looked inside—a circumference of pink on the bottom was all that remained of his strawberry shake.

The boy in the blue "LUCKY" t-shirt said something to the most attractive girl in the group of high schoolers, and everyone cracked up laughing. Dewey was not in on the joke. (He never was.) And he did not know the "LUCKY" scrawled across the boy's chest was not meant to be taken as an adjective, but was merely a popular fashion label.

LUCKY, Dewey thought. Max Buras. My little Max. Talisman. Madam Hagar. Boise, Idaho.

Maybe Dewey would stop in Boise.

❈ ❈ ❈

Already Dewey looked different than when he'd arrived in Boise; he'd decided to shave his head after a chance run-in with a guy who was sporting a buzz cut at the YMCA sauna.

"I wasn't fooling anyone anymore with all the artful comb-over," the man said as he and Dewey sat on the plank-wood bench, each of them sweating profusely and wearing towels around their waists.

The guy had looked at his bare feet then, as if Dewey might take offense, but Dewey got the message loud and clear. He had made a bee line from the Y showers to the North End Barbershop, where he'd paid $14, $15 with tip, to get the same haircut he'd seen on the guy in the sauna.

Now, knocking around his room at the Grandview, and catching a glimpse of himself in the mirror, he wondered whether or not he could scare up enough money to buy new teeth. Growing up he'd never had much in the way of dental care on account of his falling through the gaps of his foster parents' insurance. One of his "brothers" had actually gone into Dewey's mouth with a pair of pliers in order to try and straighten him out, which had only made things worse. New teeth would cost $2,450, according to a guy he'd known back at the garage in Oregon. He wasn't sure if that was before or after insurance, which he still didn't have, and so far he'd made only around $750 at the video poker. He wondered whether or not it would hurt, like the pliers, to get new teeth.

The TV still had rabbit ears and, as far as Dewey could tell, no remote. He kept it on, anyway, just for the company. Federal Way was a busy piece of road and he could hear the hum of traffic even through the closed door to his room.

He wondered about his future in Boise.

Madam Hagar—Psychic Medium for Apparitions, Poltergeists, and all things Paranormal—answered on the second ring.

"You found your talisman," she said. "Or it found you?"

"HE found me," Dewey said. "A boy. Max."

"Max," she repeated.

"Yeah. And yes, I found him, or he found me, whatever. A distant relative—I remembered him from an old Christmas card, his t-shirt: LUCKY. Said the word right there on the front of his shirt, plain as day."

"So you figured he was the talisman," Madam Hagar said.

"Of course. Wouldn't you?"

"Maybe you're the lucky one," she said. Dewey held his handsome new cellular telephone away from his ear and looked at it. "Sorry, we must have a bad connection. Did you say I'm the lucky one?"

Madam Hagar sighed deeply. "Maybe *you're* the one who saved *him*," she said. "Just when you think you know, you'll be reminded you don't know a thing. You're in for a surprise."

"I don't think you understand," Dewey said. "He's the lucky one. I've been bringing him with me to play the video poker—I've been winning for a change."

"You're using him for your own financial gain?"

Dewey felt his spirits sink. "Uh. Yes?"

"Interesting," Madam Hagar said. "I imagined you might aspire to a higher purpose."

Dewey's mind raced. "What do you mean, maybe I saved him? I mean, don't get me wrong, I'd like to save him, if he needs saving, but—"

"I don't think you were quite listening the last time we spoke: 'You will find a talisman,' I told you, but don't worry about turning over stones because in addition, I said, 'It will find you.'"

Dewey rubbed his temples with his thumb and forefinger; suddenly he had another headache.

"Perhaps you didn't get my meaning," she continued.

"I still don't get your meaning."

"I am speaking of bio-harmonic convergence," she said.

"Yeah," Dewey said, "and that's the problem. I'm waiting for you to start speaking English."

"You are lucky," Madam Hagar said, "for each other. Bio-harmonic convergence. As long as you continue to be in contact with your talisman, whoever he, she or it is, then this will continue to be so."

Dewey held the phone out in front of him again. *You are lucky for each other.* How had he not thought of that? It explained how Dewey had suddenly started to win casino games, and how Max had correctly guessed the number of M&M candies on his teacher's desk.

"How do you know this?" he asked.

"My dear," she said. "I am Madam Hagar. I know more than you can fathom."

❋ ❋ ❋

Dewey hadn't hung up with Madam Hagar for more than 10 minutes when Max called. "I'm grounded," he said.

"What for?"

"For smoking," Max said. "Or telling my parents I've been smoking. They didn't believe me that Andy had taken up the habit."

Dewey let himself fall back on his new, creaky, slightly too soft queen size bed. "Geez. Sorry about that."

"Yeah," Max said. "Well. It's all right. They don't think I really smoke, anyway. I'm guessing they just don't like that they have no idea what's going on and I'm not telling them. I didn't really care about trick-or-treating this year anyway."

"No! That ain't fair!" Dewey wondered what kind of an adult would ground a kid for Halloween. "When is that, anyway?"

"Tomorrow."

"How long they get you for? How long you gonna be—*grounded?*"

"Three weeks," Max said.

"Oh, shit! I mean shoot," Dewey said. His conversation with Madam Hagar flooded back to him. Bio-harmonic convergence. *As long as you continue to be in contact.* How was he supposed to make enough money to buy new teeth now?

"I'm going to have to get a job," Dewey said.

"I guess," Max said. "You were working when we met. The tow truck?"

Dewey's mind flashed back to Sonny's towing, and then to the YMCA.

48

On his way to the locker room sauna, he'd seen a flier posting an open janitorial position of "with medical-dental benefits." *Medical-Dental.* New teeth. He'd have to fill out a background check, but maybe he could finesse that the way he had in Oregon.

"Hey," Dewey said, "you know what the most disgusting job on earth is?"

Max laughed. "No. What?"

"Mixed martial arts mop man," Dewey said. "I had a friend did that back in Oregon. Guy had to wear latex on his latex, all the stuff that's out there in blood these days—AIDS and Ebola. Yuck!"

"Gross," Max said. "That sounds terrible. Maybe get a different job than that one."

"Oh, I almost forgot to tell you," Dewey said, "we're in bio-harmonic convergence."

"What's that mean?"

"Yeah, I asked the same thing," Dewey said. "Apparently it means we're each other's good luck charms. Those M&M's? The lucky golf balls?"

"You mean that was—that was YOU?"

"Guess so," Dewey said.

"But you weren't even there."

Now it was Dewey who laughed. "I don't need to be. Apparently it's enough that we're just hanging out together. I think if we don't hang out, we must eventually wear off or something—the magic, or luck, or whatever, it must just—evaporate."

"Says who?"

"Madam Hagar."

"The psychic you told me about?" Max said.

"Yeah," Dewey said. "Madam Hagar."

"So I don't need to actually be right next to you, breathing on your quarters?"

"I'm guessing it probably doesn't hurt," Dewey said. "I'd prefer it if you were, since that's my main source of income. Or was my main source of income."

There was a long silence on Max's end.

"What's your birthday?" he finally said.

More silence, this time on Dewey's end.

"C'mon," Max pushed, "what's your birthday?"

"Who cares?" Dewey cringed at the defensiveness in his voice. "I mean, what's that got to do with the price of tea in China, you know what I mean?"

"It's a simple question," Max said. "What if we were born on the same day, or even at the same time on the same day? Not the same year, obviously, but that might begin to explain—"

"I don't know it," Dewey said.

"That's okay, I don't know the time, either, but that's a thing we can find—"

"I don't know my birthday," Dewey said. This was how it always went when he told people. They couldn't believe it. Or they started feeling sorry for him, or like he was some kind of alien species. Max was no different. Dewey could hear it in the silence.

"Hello?"

"Wow. Well, uh, yeah, I'm here," Max said. "We gotta find out your birthday, Dewey. Right? I mean, you get more presents if you know your birthday."

"Guess so," Dewey said.

"So anyway," Max continued, "me being grounded and all that, I guess I'll call you around Thanksgiving, or just before. You'll stay?"

"Stay in town?"

"Yeah," Max said. "Stay in town."

"Heck, yeah!" Dewey said. "I just got a new place! Besides, I got a coupla' irons in the fire." Actually he had just one iron, and it wasn't yet in the fire, but the janitorial job sounded pretty sweet. *Full medical-dental.*

"I'll talk to you in three weeks," Dewey said. "Do good in school."

"Okay."

Dewey felt a sudden chill. If the job at the Y fell through, he was going to wind up back on the streets. "Hey, I almost forgot to ask," he said. "If you're not allowed to trick or treat, are you at least allowed to dress up for Halloween?"

"Yeah," Max said. "Of course."

"Well? What are you going to be?"

CHAPTER

Max placed the phone back in its receiver in the living room—a cell phone, like LASIK surgery, seemed to be a luxury reserved only for older kids like his sister, just his luck.

It all made sense now, how he, Max, had never before been lucky until now. He'd simply never run across Dewey Tomlinson, and Dewey Tomlinson had never run across Max Buras. They were like the two main characters in that old movie Max's parents had made the family watch, E.T. The wrinkly little alien guy, E.T., and the little boy, who looked sort of like Gabe, started acting like they shared the same internal circuitry. If one started dying, the other started dying, too; and if the first one started feeling better, the other started to rebound.

Max couldn't remember how it had all ended, but somehow the little wrinkly alien had wound up getting beamed up back to his home planet, and somehow it involved "phoning home."

Max and Dewey; Dewey and Max. Bio-harmonic convergence. There was only one thing that didn't make sense: How could a guy not know his own birthday?

Max looked at the huge, red numbers on his clock radio—the only clock radio they'd ever found with numbers big enough for his uncorrected vision: 8:23.

Gabe was out in the living room, playing with Mars. Their parents were in the TV room with the door closed. Sadie was with Graham Godwin at the Halloween Dance, which was held one day before Halloween so as not to interfere with trick or treating. Susannah Jurevicious was also at the Halloween Dance, with Bridge Academy's No. 1 golfer, Pete Whiting. But Max tried not to think about this.

✻ ✻ ✻

Sadie was wearing her fancy, turquoise underwear from Victoria's Secret under her costume; it had cost her a lot, this underwear. And it wasn't like she had the money to burn anymore, either. Thanks to the crummy luck of having run into stupid "Uncle Dewey" in the mall, she was no longer receiving a kickback from Max's illicit gambling winnings.

In any event, she was here now. She'd put some thought into her costume, and her mother had helped. She was supposed to be Katy Perry, but all evening people kept asking if she was a Playboy bunny, which was embarrassing. It was like she had forgotten a crucial part of the costume, a boom box or something that could play a soundtrack of Katy songs just to clue people in that she wasn't trying to look like some crummy centerfold.

Graham Godwin was an okay dancer, if a little wooden. His go-to move seemed to involve throwing his head back and churning his arms as if he was a long-distance runner. Sadie was almost thankful for the slow songs, since those seemed to lessen the odds of Graham injuring himself or Sadie. He could relax his flailing arms and simply let his hands rest on Sadie's hips, which she didn't mind.

It was during Justin Timberlake's "Not a Bad Thing," which everyone seemed to have decided was a slow-dance song, that Graham kissed her. At 16, he was shaving now, but not shaving very well; his stubbly whiskers dug into Sadie's lips, and she reflexively pulled away.

"Your whiskers," she said. Even in the semi-darkness she could see he looked hurt.

"Just not so hard," she said, and he moved in again, pressing himself into her mouth. He tasted like beer.

They all went to Missy McGrath's afterward. Graham drove his Chevy Suburban, and they packed the three rows of bench seats with kids and peeled away from Bridge Academy, the tires squealing and most likely leaving some rubber on the road.

It took them about 10 minutes to get there, during which time Graham drove like a lunatic, much to the amusement, apparently, of everyone in the car but Sadie.

Missy lived in a big house up in the foothills, and her parents seemed to be gone, perhaps on a trip, and everyone was drinking punch that tasted to Sadie like it had alcohol in it. She wasn't sure what kind. The music was loud, and angry, and she and Graham wound up making out in an unoccupied guest bedroom. Sadie's skin felt as hot as a skillet as she took her top off, revealing her turquoise Victoria's Secret bra, which she felt certain Graham would appreciate. He would recognize her for the mature and alluring adult that she was, and somehow this would elevate him, too, waking him up to the fact that he was a man now.

But he made no comment—until he did.

"Take it off," he said.

Sadie's face fell. Take it off? Did he realize the lengths she'd gone to just to be able to put it on? Did he realize this satin bra was the product of a fifty-dollar, exceptionally covert and, thanks to Dewey, exceptionally embarrassing and extra costly excursion to the mall?

"Come on, I said take it off," he said again.

Sadie had had exactly three sips of the spiked punch, but suddenly she felt sick.

How old are you?

Fifteen.

Age inappropriate!

Good decisions, girls.

She had to get out of here. Not because of Dewey, no. She had to get out of there not because he was afraid or she was afraid or anyone was afraid, but because she might do something she would regret for the rest of her life. She had to get out of there because of Graham, handsome Graham, silly Graham, immature Graham, *rude* Graham. Rude. That's what he was.

Sadie broke away from his gaze and eyed her brown halter top in a crumpled heap and walked over to the bed.

"That's what I'm talking about," Graham said, his eyes following her across the room.

She slipped her top on.

"What are you doing?" he asked. "I want to see the centerfold!"

"I told you, I'm not a Playboy bunny," she said, opening the door and finger-combing her hair. "I'm Katy Perry! Goodbye, Graham. Have a nice party! Have a nice life!" She slammed the door behind her, which felt kind of good and terrible at the same time.

※ ※ ※

Max sighed and looked down at the orange and blue throw rug in his room.

If there was one good thing about being grounded it was that Max had an excellent excuse for not going to tonight's Halloween dance, besides being unpopular, which was pretty embarrassing, as excuses go.

Still, Andy had not been pleased to learn that Max, on account of being grounded, wouldn't be trick or treating the next day. They'd been Halloween buddies practically forever.

"You can come over here," Max told him. "We'll hand out candy to tiny Wolverines and Spidermen. It'll be fun. We're getting too old to go out, anyway."

"Yeah," Andy said.

Now, though, Max felt his mood darken. Did he really want to stay at home and hand out candy like an adult? He wouldn't get to feel the weight of his pillowcase increase from house to house, or trade candy through the night, or trick or treat at Susannah Jurevicious's house, or stow his candy where no one would find it and snack on it for weeks if not months.

He walked into the hallway bathroom and stared at the mirror. He didn't look too old to trick or treat.

Their parents never came in here, they had their own bathroom, and maybe that was why they seemed blissfully unaware of one of the most useful quirks in the house, which Max decided must be some sort of engineering flaw but which he was in no hurry to reveal to his parents.

From the hallway bathroom, without the water running, one could hear, with alarming accuracy, conversations in the TV room—provided the TV was off. The two rooms shared a wall—a porous wall. Max heard the soft echo of his parents' voices and moved to the flowery wallpaper. He cupped his ear with his hand.

"There have to be consequences, that's all I'm saying." His dad.

"Yes, and we've done that. We've punished him." His mom.

"Beyond that, though. He lied to us about Andy, and now he's lied to us about his own smoking. I have to admit, I didn't think the little guy had it in him, but now that he's started lying he doesn't seem to be able to stop. There is no way he's suddenly started smoking."

"Well, what's the explanation, then?" His mom again.

"Beats me. Those bowling alleys *can* be smoky, that's true, but I'm sorry, I just can't see Max happening upon a mostly empty pack of cigarettes and deciding he should bring them home because—he wants to try one? No. That's not Max. That's not our son."

"Don't you think we're taking our eye off the ball?" His mom again. "Max isn't the one we need to worry about, and neither is Sadie. Gabe is 10 and he's not talking. He can't even say his own name. He wanders around like—"

"We've been over this! Steve says we've got to just give him space. It could just be developmental. We're doing all we can with Cynthia."

"Or he could be—" But his mom didn't finish the thought. Max pressed his ear up to the bathroom wall a little harder.

There was nothing further.

Max came away from the wall and took off his glasses and looked in the mirror. He had Gabe's eyes, Gabe's freckled complexion and the same sort of widow's peak above his forehead. But where God had remembered to include all the parts, to follow most of the directions when building Max Buras, he'd forgotten something when constructing Gabe.

Max quietly let himself out of the bathroom.

Gabe was right where Max had left him in the living room, curled up on the couch with Mars, who wasn't supposed to be up there but who pretty much lived on that couch like he owned the deed. Gabe wore jeans with the zipper down, and a too-big, light-blue sweatshirt, handed down from Max, with white letters: LUCKY.

Gabe scratched Mars' tummy and hummed softly, rocking back and forth in the couch. Max eyed his parents, still in conference, grim-faced, behind the closed glass door to the TV room, and sat down on the other side of Mars. Gabe did not look up. Max took hold of Gabe's hand, gently lifting it off Mars's pink belly, and Gabe reflexively tried to pull away but Max didn't let go. His little brother lifted his chin, his eyes registering Max's presence before quickly looking away.

"G-a-a-a-b-e," Max said.

"Gabe," Max said again. "That's your name. Say your name. Can you say your name? Say your name, Gabe. G-a-a-a-b-e. Come on, you can do it."

Gabe looked down at the dog and continued humming, rocking back and forth on the couch. Mars looked at Gabe, then at Max, as if to ask if someone was going to get his belly scratched or maybe a Milk Bone or at least a short walk.

Dr. Steve, Max's mother and father, the pretty speech therapist Cynthia—all of them had tried the same thing, in pretty much the same way. But none of them had been his brother, and Max couldn't recall whether any of them had tried it exactly this way, holding Gabe's hand. Plus, Max now had special powers, after all.

"G-a-a-a-b-e," Max said again. "Gabe."

Nothing. Gabe tried to pull his hand away, and Max let him.

"Gabe," Max said.

Gabe's curled, delicate fingers come to rest again on Mars's pink belly, and Mars, balancing on his tiny backbone, paws in the air, offered a contented sigh. Max shifted his weight forward on the couch before getting to his feet. He felt his lower lip trembling again, the hot tears pooling up again, and he didn't want to upset his brother.

"Gabe," Max said again. Their parents were still in the TV room, the TV off, deep in conversation. *It's hopeless*, Max thought. *You're wasting your breath. Your brother is as mute as a post, as dumb as a box of hammers. He'll never talk. Never. Never. Never.*

CHAPTER

Max slept fitfully. He woke up, parted his curtains and looked out into the cold sunshine, and decided not to go to school in costume even though it was now officially Halloween.

That turned out to be a good call, because at 1:14 p.m., in fifth period Spanish class, Susannah Jurevicious spun around in her seat and asked him if he had an extra pencil.

"Yes!" Max said.

"Ay, silencio," Mr. Raymundo said.

"Okaaaaay," Susannah said under her breath.

Max rummaged through his backpack, thoughts firing madly in his head. She could've asked anyone for a pencil—Freddy Robinson in front of her; Grace Hester or Julia Ackworth to her left and right, respectively—but she had asked Max. What did that mean? Did it mean anything? Did she think he was good looking? Or at least cute? Boys seemed to find his sister good looking, and he was closely related to Sadie, after all. He tried to run a quick math equation in his head: If A, then B, if B, then C, but then maybe the law of hypothetical syllogism or the transitive property or whatever this was did not apply. Did Susannah Jurevicious know his name? Surely she knew his name.

"Thanks," Susannah said as he handed her a No. 2 Dixon Ticonderoga with a serviceable point. She turned around to face the front of the room.

Max looked down at the words on his travel-vocabulary quiz, which had blurred into an incomprehensible mush of letters and squiggly eyebrows. *Donde esta el bano?* His ears were on fire, and he could hear his pulse. His neck felt red enough to fry an egg. Had she winked at him? No. As much as he replayed her quick, perfunctory thank you, as much as he ran it back across his frontal cortex frame by frame, he could detect no wink.

But wait—what did she think of him? Did he, Max, look like the type of guy who not only remembered to bring his own school supplies to class, he brought extras for anyone else who might've forgotten theirs? And if he did look like that type of guy, was that a good thing or a bad thing? Max looked down at the test on his desk, unmarked by Max's hand. Good gawd, boy, get it together! You've got a test to take!

She had smiled, though. There was that. It was a smile that could quicken the blood, stir the soul and make a man believe in something again. Wait. Had he heard that on a diamond commercial? No, no, he'd just made that up. Heck, that was pretty good!

She had not come to school dressed as Elvira; instead, she wore a reddish Stanford sweatshirt and snug jeans. Max was thankful, looking around the room, that he hadn't worn his Halloween costume to school. How on earth was he ever going to get Susannah Jurevicious to go out with him if he looked like a Minion? Far better, he'd reasoned that morning, just to go with the Los Angeles Lakers jersey Andy had given him, explaining that Max's goggles made him look like a much shorter and much whiter version of a Los Angeles Laker named Lew Alcindor and then Kareem Abdul-Jabbar.

Susannah's hair smelled as fragrant and looked as spectacular as ever, if a bit messier than usual. Max considered himself an expert on the matter. He wondered how late she'd stayed out the night before, at the Halloween dance, with the swine Pete Whiting. Or perhaps, and maybe this was wishful thinking, that tired look on the face of Susannah Jurevicious was from having stayed up all night crying and talking it out with her best friend, Zoe Allenby. Maybe Susannah and Pete Whiting had broken up.

"I'll tell you what you've got to do to get girls," Dewey had told Max one day during a lull in the video poker action. "You either play a varsity sport, or you become a rock star, or, barring that, you do theater. Knowing you, I suggest option three."

"Just wait it out, buddy," his dad had told him. "Nothing lasts forever, especially not at this age. That goes for relationships and, uh, the quote-unquote *awkward* phase."

Max had a feeling he was going to have to wait a long, long time. And he didn't think he was the type to get involved in the theater arts, like his sister.

❀ ❀ ❀

Andy came over at six, dressed as a hobo.

"Will work for candy," his cardboard sign said.

"Good one," Max said.

He looked down at his yellow Minion shirt through his Minion glasses, which were merely his own glasses but with a new, perfectly round black circumference stuck to each lens.

"How'd you guys do that?" Andy asked, getting up in Max's face to inspect the glasses.

"My mom," Max said. "Duct tape—it was tricky making it perfectly round like that—I think she had to use a protractor or something."

Max's mother had baked a casserole that everyone ate quickly before the group broke apart. Sadie was bound for yet another party, this time at Lilly Robinson's house. Max's mother and father were out escorting Gabe, dressed as Darth Vader, on a quick trip around the neighborhood.

"You two will be okay on your own?" Max's mom asked.

"We got this," Andy said.

"Don't worry, Mom," Max added. "It's kids and candy. What could go wrong?"

Well, it wasn't really candy. Max's mom was that neighborhood mom who, instead of handing out miniature Snickers and KitKats, handed out miniature mandarines, and raisins in tiny, green boxes. Max looked into the giant wooden salad bowl and fished around with his fingers. The closest things to candy were individually wrapped, four-sided, sesame-and-honey sticks about the size of his little finger. Max rolled his eyes as Andy unwrapped one.

"Not bad," he said, mid-chew, as Max's parents and brother closed the front door behind them. "But the rest of this stuff." He swallowed and looked down into the salad bowl full of orange orbs and little, green boxes of raisins. He shook his head. "You're going to need to have a talk with your mom. This stuff—I mean, geez, Max, let's be honest, this stuff isn't doing your rep any favors. My mom is a health nut, but at least she springs for some chocolate on Halloween. It's dark chocolate—she says it's actually healthy—but at least it's chocolate. It's not *Cutie* mandarins."

"Yeah," Max said. "I know. You'd think I'd be used to it."

Dinner wasn't bad, all things considered. There was no dessert. They ate sesame-and-honey sticks while greeting tiny gremlins, ghosts and ninjas at the door.

"C'mon, let's go get some *real* candy," some kid said as he made a quick exit from their front stoop. He was dressed as Wolverine, and Max felt a shame bomb detonate in his chest. He could hardly blame the kid, who was only voicing what most were probably thinking. Little kids were great that way; honest to a fault.

Max and Andy had worked their way through most of the sesame-and-honey sticks and very few mandarins and raisin boxes when his parents came back with Gabe.

"Honey, the Thuernagles are having a thing," his mom said.

"Okay," Max said.

"And your father and I would like to go. Do you mind if Gabe stays with you?"

She plopped her purse on the kitchen counter, and Max wondered why she'd felt the need to bring it. His father looked at his watch. Gabe had his Vader mask under his left arm, and a respectable bulge at the bottom of the pillowcase in his right.

"Yep," Max said. "I mean no, I don't mind. Good haul, Gabe!"

His brother said nothing as he walked in and sat down on the couch to sort through his candy.

"We'll be back in about 20," his mom said. "We just want to make a quick appearance."

"Just in and out," his dad said.

"Take your time," Max said. "We got it under control here, right Gabe?"

Gabe said nothing. He dumped out his pillowcase full of candy onto the couch and began sifting through it, occasionally stopping to unwrap a piece and eat it.

Their mother looked at this and winced.

"Okay, well we'll see you three later," she said, closing the door behind them.

"Get anything good, Gabe?" Andy asked.

But there was no answer, as ever, because Gabe was in Gabe Land, and as Max and his mother knew all the sugar was going to take him even farther away than normal.

※ ※ ※

The flow of trick-or-treaters, so steady an hour ago, had been reduced to more of an irregular drip when the buzzer sounded and Andy opened the door to find someone dressed as Gru, with the black pants, gray sport coat, black-and-gray scarf, and giant Gru head, under which was someone who had to be at least six feet tall. Minions, Max knew, were the stars of *Despicable Me*, but Gru was the film's second most famous character.

Andy invited the guy inside. "Hey, Max, check it out!"

"Happy Halloween," said the guy, Gru. "Uh, I mean, trick or treat."

His voice was familiar, and Max felt his eyes bug out of his head. "Uncle Dewey?"

Dewey Tomlinson pried his giant Gru head off his sweaty head and smiled sheepishly. "Hi," he said. "Geez, it's hot as blazes in there."

"Whoa," Andy said.

"You're not supposed to be here!" Max said in a loud whisper before remembering that his parents were not in the house. Not yet, anyway. "You're going to get me grounded for the rest of my life! What if my parents find you here? I mean my mom knows you but my dad doesn't, and won't you have to sort of explain yourself, and I'm terrible at keeping a secret, and what if they find out about all the gambling?"

How long had they been gone? Ten minutes? Twenty?

"Oh, calm down, they're not here," Dewey said. "I waited for them to leave." He had a cigarette in his mouth and was fumbling with his lighter.

"No!" Max said. "Not here! Put that away!"

Dewey did.

"What are you doing here?"

"It's Halloween," Dewey said.

"I know! But why are you on my doorstep? You're going to get us both busted!"

Dewey shrugged. "Bio-harmonic convergence? I thought maybe we could, you know, recharge the mojo. My luck's been running a little cold. Plus I thought you might need me to put out another homework fire." He smiled hopefully, but no one laughed.

Andy looked confused. "What's this about a bio-harmonic homework fire?"

"You've got to go," Max said.

"Let's at least take a picture first," Dewey said.

Max opened the door and poked his head out to look for his parents. "Okay, but let's not take all day. Come on, come on—let's do it fast. Andy? Phone?"

Dewey stepped into the foyer, where the light was better. Andy whipped out his cell phone and Dewey threw his Gru head back on as he and Max clasped their raised hands like they were on the Olympic podium or something. Max felt something take hold of his free hand, and looked down to see a tiny Darth Vader without his helmet: Gabe.

"Gabe," Max said, the middle link of the chain between Dewey and Gabe.

"Max," Gabe said, looking up at his brother.

"This tall man here is Dewey," Max said, nodding at Dewey, but he did a double take. His head snapped back and he looked down onto Gabe, then Andy.

"Wait," Max said. "Did he just say my name? Did Gabe just say my name? Gabe, did you just say my name?"

"Yeah!" Andy said, the blood having drained from his face, too. "Yes!"

"Gabe," Max said, feeling his breath catch.

"Max," Gabe said.

Max raised his and Gabe's and Dewey's arms toward the sky, all three of them now on the Olympic podium: gold, silver and bronze.

"My brother is talking!" Max said. "My brother is talking!"

"Whoa!" Andy said.

"What? What's happening?" Dewey said through his giant Gru head. "I can't see a thing in here!"

Max laughed. "Gabe!" he said.

"Max!" Gabe said.

"Why do you guys keep saying each other's names?" Dewey asked, his voice muffled under his sweaty fake head.

"Gabe!" Max said again.

"Max!" Gabe repeated.

"Yes!" Max said. "Yes! Yes! Yes!"

Then their parents showed up.

CHAPTER 13

Dewey couldn't sleep. He closed his eyes, opened them again, closed them again, and listened to the road noise on Federal Way outside his room at the Grandview Motel. It had been three days since he'd last seen Max, and Dewey's spirits were low as he wondered just exactly what it was he was doing here in Boise, Idaho.

Video poker was out. Without Max by his side, all he did was lose. And that included even his favorite machine at Emerald Lanes – *Five Aces!* at Emerald Lanes. It was hard to believe it had been only four days since they were all dancing around Max's living room, delirious over his brother's speech breakthrough, or whatever it was. Their celebration had been short-lived, though, with the arrival of their parents and all of them hastily explaining that Dewey was just a really tall kid in a Gru costume who had insisted on taking a picture with the Minion before slipping out the door.

Dewey wondered if they'd bought it. He wouldn't have. He noticed his cousin Judy, Max's mom, had put on a few worry lines around her face since he'd last seen her.

Keep busy. That was Dewey's credo for when things weren't going well, and he'd done a pretty good job of keeping busy. Hospital records in Seattle showed Dwight "Dewey" Tomlinson to be 44 years old, which when he thought about it, sounded just about right. He was born May 14, 1971, and this had not been the easiest information to find. In fact it had been tedious work. He'd had to call one main number, followed by another, and he was transferred, until he'd finally happened upon the woman he apparently was supposed to have called in the first place. Alas, this person was on break and he went to voicemail.

When he finally got the information he'd been seeking, Dewey wrote it down on a slip of paper and tucked the paper into his wallet, behind the colorful business card for Madam Hagar. Damned if he was going to go through all those phone calls again.

Police records would tell much of the rest of his life story, or at least his life story before "the mistake," as he called it, as if he'd done nothing more serious than buy the wrong kind of orange juice at the grocery store, although you didn't do seven and a half years at the Walls for buying the wrong kind of orange juice. You didn't need a trial, a trip to Walla Walla to sit on death row for a while, and intervention from the Northwest Innocence Project, a change of lawyers, and another trial just to get back on the bricks.

His first lawyer had been disbarred. His second lawyer, the one who had saved Dewey Tomlinson from living the rest of his life behind bars, had wound up on the cover of *Time* magazine. But neither of these men was burned into the deepest folds of Dewey's brain. On nights like this, when he couldn't sleep, Dewey sometimes saw the man confronting him under the bridge, those eyes so full of rage and confusion.

"I'm sorry," Dewey said. "I'm so, so sorry."

❀ ❀ ❀

He gave up. He turned on the light, looked down at the giant book from Barnes & Noble on his nightstand: *The Secret Science of Birthday Numerology, Astrology, and Personality.* He couldn't believe he'd gone so long without even knowing his birthday. There were all sorts of things, apparently, that a guy could do and know if he just committed those digits to memory, the exact day and month and year that he'd popped out onto the stage and delivered his opening monologue. (Dewey assumed, given what he'd seen on TV and in the movies, that his opening monologue had been a bunch of nonsensical burbling and deeply annoying shrieking and crying.)

For one thing, he could now get a free meal at Denny's—or at least he could get a legitimate free meal, one he could feel good about eating. He had had to have a birthday, of course, when he'd applied for a driver's license. He'd had to have an up-to-date license to work for Sonny's Roadside Towing in Oregon. But until now he'd had to work with a made-up birthday, a date that had been given to him after he'd persuaded the powers that be that no one really knew, that there were no parents or grandparents to ask, the foster mother didn't know, and the hospital where he was born had burned to the ground. (Dewey had had to make a LOT of calls to get around that particular glitch.)

The other thing a guy could do if he knew his real birthday was what Madam Hagar suggested he do: consult the book on his nightstand. Buying it had seemed impractical, given that Dewey had never been much of a reader and the book was as expensive as it was heavy, but he'd bucked up and done it anyway. He sat up in bed, carefully hoisted the book into his lap, and turned to May 14.

The good news was he shared a birthday with George Lucas, the guy who made all those Star Wars movies, and Rob Gronkowski, a pretty dynamite football player. The bad news was the book predicted general turbulence and, "an ongoing battle to maintain stability." That didn't seem so great, but hell, it sure seemed accurate.

Dewey's mind raced as he skimmed down the long entry, and that's when he saw it, the part that stopped him cold: "The best way for those born on this day to mitigate against aforementioned instability is to ally themselves with others also born on this day. In fact, the planets suggest such joining of forces may lead to a powerful alchemy."

Dewey's reread the passage, his heart thumping wildly. His life made sense in a way it never had before, the last two-plus months of M&M's and highly productive poker, for he knew who else shared his birthday and that would explain everything.

CHAPTER

The Treasure Valley District Championship was held at Hillcrest Country Club in Boise, in a driving, cold rain.

Max looked up at the dark skies as the guys tried to warm up on the driving range, where it really would be possible only to cool down, to freeze, to contract hypothermia. November 3 was way too late to have scheduled this thing, but while he normally would have stayed warm and dry while doing his homework in the clubhouse, Max felt the occasion demanded he at least make a show of support out on the course.

Mr. Raymundo apparently did not share Max's opinion. Hands in his pockets, hood pulled down low over his forehead, the Bridge golf coach was so bundled up he looked like he was ready to summit Everest. He turned and headed for the clubhouse.

Max's feet were already wet. His glasses were hopelessly foggy; he could barely see down to the dark and light blue sleeves of his rain suit, which was made by the same company whose gear had leaked at the 2010 Ryder Cup golf matches in Wales. (Max was dry. Clearly they'd fixed the problem.)

He hadn't had it in him to keep messing with Pete Whiting's game—and helping his teammates—after the one time against Star Christian. Whiting didn't deserve it. He hadn't done anything to Max, or at least he hadn't done anything to Max that everyone else didn't do—mostly take him for granted.

Water pooled up on Max's floppy-brimmed hat—ball caps, like all the other kids wore, did not fit his peanut-shaped head—and dripped onto his shoulders as he watched the boys hit a few balls on the driving range.

It felt like someone was tapping him as if to tell him something, and for some reason this made him think of Gabe, and "the miracle," as Max thought of it now, three days earlier. Gabe—who had talked.

Max and Andy hastily had ushered Dewey out the door, passing him off as a trick-or-treater, and in all the commotion Gabe had locked up again and stopped talking.

"But Mom, Dad, you've got to believe me," Max said. "He was talking. He said my name. He said 'Max.' He kept saying 'Max.' Go ahead, Gabe, go ahead and say it again. *Max*."

Gabe hummed to himself, head down, as he rummaged through his pillowcase of candy.

"Andy?" their mother said.

"It's true, Mrs. B. He said 'Max.' I heard him."

"Huh," Max's father said. He was still looking at the door that had closed behind Dewey.

❋ ❋ ❋

According to the rumors, either Pete Whiting or Hadley Jackson's dad, or both, had convinced someone at Hillcrest Country Club it would be a good idea to "grow the game" and all that jazz by hosting the district's all-important, end-of-the-season 18-hole championship. That was twice the number of holes as at a normal tournament or match, since anyone could get hot over nine holes and the goal here was to identify "Champion Golfer of the Fall," and not just some flash in the pan—not just some kid who got *lucky*.

There it was—that word again.

Maybe, Max thought, Alan Whiting wasn't such a lousy guy, after all.

Max had not spent the day with his jacket pockets full of golf balls, keeping them warm and full of good bounces or whatever he thought he'd done before—whatever he *had* done before. He suspected it wouldn't have been much use to the team, anyway. The golf balls would just get cold and wet, anyway, in all this crummy weather. Max had not had any contact with Dewey in three days, and not much contact before that.

Even if he discounted today's monsoon, Max felt like after approximately two months of happy kismet and fine fortune, he was finally running out of luck. Maybe Dewey was right. Maybe the bio-harmonic convergence pump needed priming.

Max had gotten a C- on his travel-vocabulary quiz in Spanish, but that had been less a function of bad luck than raging hormones and his totally embarrassing inability to get himself together after Susannah Jurevicius had asked him for a pencil. Now Mr. Raymundo would think him incapable of asking for directions if he ever got lost in Barcelona, even though Max knew perfectly well how to say not just "left" and "right," but also, "Where can I get a good cup of coffee?"—Mr. Raymundo was a pretty avid coffee drinker—and, after the coffee, "Where is the bathroom?"

There were other signs that Max's luck had run dry. His bike had flatted out two days in a row, both times on the rear wheel, while biking to school. And if it was getting too cold to bike to school in Idaho, it was definitely getting too cold to change a tire. His vision seemed to be going from bad to worse. An angry pimple had taken up residence just above the bridge of his nose, and when he tried to hide it by adjusting his goggles his lenses went out of focus causing some kind of weird light refraction thing.

The guys finished warming up and Max made his way to the first tee, where, for the first time all season, he would cede the announcing duties to someone else.

The first-tee announcer turned out to be some old, snowy-haired guy from the IHSAA who had no microphone—which might have been a problem in the rain, anyway—and who kept clearing his throat and holding his clipboard up to his face as if the ink was running in the rain, which it probably was.

"The 11:46 starting time"—ahem, cough, ahem, he brought the clipboard up to his nose—"from Bridge Academy, Peter Whiting!"

The only person in the gallery, Max clapped, but he stopped when Pete Whiting whirled around and shot him an icy glare. Bridge Academy's No. 1 golfer then stood up to his ball, reared back as much as his rain suit allowed, and hooked his drive into a pond.

Hillcrest's short, par-4 opener was a cupcake of a hole, really, unless you did precisely what Whiting had just done, in which case birdie was out of the equation, par was going to be a challenge, and bogey was the most likely outcome.

"Damn it!" Whiting said.

The IHSAA old timer looked down at his tee sheet, pretending not to have heard the breach of etiquette. He announced the Mountain View player, whose ball forged a true path through the icy rain and pelted the fairway despite what to Max had seemed like a funky swing. The Star Christian kid, no doubt trying too hard to avoid Whiting's mistake and thus overcorrecting for the threat of water, hit into the right rough.

"Gentlemen, best of luck today," the old guy said.

The three strapped their golf bags over their shoulders and trudged down the hill, where Whiting would have to take a drop and hit his third shot from the edge of the lake—a lousy way to begin what was sure to be a crappy day.

Standing out in the rain, Max found himself sort of wishing his dad hadn't made "an exception for school functions" amid what was initially described as a three-week period of being grounded. Even in his thick mittens he could no longer feel the tips of his fingers. According to the weather forecast guy, Lyin' Larry, there was a 40 percent chance of snow. The remote-control, miniature airplanes that swooped and climbed and dove from the glider port just off the 18th fairway—by far Gabe's favorite part about golf, the one time he'd seen them— were nowhere in sight. Even the birds seemed to have been grounded.

After watching the remaining Bridge Academy golfers tee off, Max retired to the clubhouse to tackle the math homework, plus the extra-credit problem. (He was still trying to get back in the good graces of Mrs. Hickenlooper.) He ate a tuna sandwich, prepared and wrapped up and stuffed into his knapsack by his mom. He bought a can of cranberry juice and Junior Mints from the vending machine. Other than the district tournament there seemed to be exactly nothing going on at the course. There were no lights on in the pro shop, and the clubhouse restaurant was closed.

Max easily tore through his math worksheets and waited, wondering what Gabe was doing at this moment, and what Susannah Jurevicious was doing, too.

Pete Whiting was the first one to blow in through the clubhouse doors, and he looked soaked to the bone. His cheeks were apple-red, his nose running, his hair wet. Drips ran down off the front of his cap and pelted the carpet.

"How'd it go?" Max asked. Whiting said nothing. He looked mad enough to kill, wet enough to have just emerged from the club's covered swimming pool.

How'd it go? Not so well, Max surmised in the loud silence as Whiting marched off toward the bathroom.

❈ ❈ ❈

It had been a fine fall for the Bridge golfers—the best ever, according to the statistics, Mr. Raymundo had reminded them more than once. There'd been a big write-up in the school paper. All of which made their scores today at districts, when it really mattered, seem even worse than they already were.

A good 18-hole score for a high school golfer was around 75 or maybe a few strokes better or worse—in general anything under 80 wasn't bad. But Whiting, the school's nominal No. 1 player, had shot 88. And for Bridge that was the highlight.

"*Ay, Dios mio,*" Mr. Raymundo said under his breath as he signed the scorecards at a card table in the clubhouse. Max knew what he meant. *Oh, my God.*

Alex Fisk had come in with an 89 and complained that he'd somehow "tweaked my neck in warm-ups." Hadley Jackson signed for a 92 and said nothing. Don Kennerly had a 95, and Phil Hendrickson had absorbed a whopping 102 strokes and was telling everyone he'd somehow left his 6-iron somewhere out on the course.

The Mountain View kid with the funny swing had shot a 76 that in the freezing rain looked like it would hold up for medalist honors. His score, like all of the scores, was written in thick, black indelible marker on a large, parchment-colored roll of paper taped to the wall, only the winning "76" was enveloped by a series of bold, red, outward-facing dashes, as if the number was exuding something—exuding victory.

Someone pointed an iPhone at the kid, and he pointed to his score and smiled as a flash went off. It looked like Mountain View would win the team title, as well.

The Bridge Academy table was quiet as a morgue.

"This will make us stronger," Mr. Raymundo said, putting on a brave face. "Tomorrow is another day. The sun will rise. Nobody died."

Max looked around at the guys, who offered no indication that they'd heard the coach. Their commiserating seemed to include a lot of hushed whispering.

"My 6-iron died," Hendrickson said. No one laughed.

The few parents who had made their way to the course gave everyone a wide berth. Hands shoved deep into pockets, they said nothing, not even Alan Whiting.

Under normal circumstances some of the guys would have gotten a ride home with those parents who had taken off from work and made their way to the course, but Max, after cleaning and stowing the clubs and wiping off his glasses, looked around the van and counted the same number of kids they'd driven here with: six, including him.

"Yo, Max," Whiting said as they pulled out of the parking lot.

Max felt his pulse quicken. "Yeah?"

"We've got some bad news."

"Yeah," said Alex, turning around to eye Max; it seemed as if Alex's sore neck, which he'd blamed for his 89, had made a miraculous recovery.

"The team has voted," Whiting said.

"Yeah," Alex said again. "The team voted."

"What, is there an echo in here?" Hadley Jackson, the team's only black player, shot a disapproving look at Alex, and then at Whiting.

"Yo," Whiting said, "it's like this: You're out."

Max suddenly felt freezing cold. "What? I'm out? What does—"

"We're voting you off the team," Whiting said. "We put it to a vote, and it was almost unanimous. You're out for the spring season."

"Three to two is *not* almost unanimous," Jackson said. "It's a joke, is what it is." Max wondered who, besides Hadley Jackson, had cast the other dissenting vote.

"Sorry, Max," Jackson said.

Max looked over at Mr. Raymundo, who changed lanes. "*Lo siento, amigo,*" he said. "Don't look at me. There's nothing I can do—it's not my team. It belongs to you all."

"So I'm just—that's it? Just like that?" Max heard his voice break, felt his lower lip quivering, the tears welling up. On, no—please don't do it. Don't cry.

"But why?" he asked when he was sure his voice wouldn't break.

No one said anything. Whiting stared out the window. He seemed to be scoping out an attractive woman as she hastily loaded up her car with groceries in the rain.

"Why?" Max asked again.

"We don't need a reason," Whiting shot back. "You're bad luck."

CHAPTER 15

Harold Buras, 45, never knew quite what to do about the fact that his youngest son, Gabe, didn't talk, and his oldest, Max, had no friends and now apparently was lying like a double agent.

And so Harold tried not to think about these things, and he found exercise helped in this regard. He looked down at his hands, his entire body shaking with exhaustion. According to Kate, the attractive but merciless leader of his "Stride" class at the YMCA, the entire month of November marked "planks-giving." Harold hated planks, and push-ups, too, for that matter.

The tall, familiar-looking guy he'd seen in the locker room circulated around the room, spraying down the equipment with sanitizer. The guy wore a YMCA polo shirt, and gave the empty, seated bench press machine a spray and a wipe. Out of the corner of his eye Harold spied the man's rather large, new look-ing hiking boots. He couldn't quite put his finger on the context, but he was fairly certain he'd seen the guy before.

"Time," Kate said.

Harold let his body fall to the floor before moving on to the next machine for lat pull-downs. The last time he'd done this class he'd barely been able to lift his arms after.

"Stay in the moment," he told himself silently, working the machine.

"Stay in the moment" had been his therapist's advice the last time they'd met. Harold had been seeing the guy for about a month and a half, and in the process had learned that he, Harold, was apparently in the midst of "a textbook mid-life crisis"—his doctor's words.

"Time," Kate said. "Assume the position!"

The entire class groaned, and Harold let his knees fall to the cool, rubber-like floor.

"Butts in the air!"

Harold planked himself, his arms shaking. His wrists felt like they might break. The janitor smelled like a combination of cleaning fluid—whatever that blue stuff was in the bottle—and cigarettes. Harold thought about the mostly empty pack of Pall Mall cigarettes he'd found in the couch cushions some five weeks earlier.

Clearly, the owner of the cigarettes had been right there in Harold's living room on Halloween night—the guy dressed, Max had to tell him later, as someone named "Gru" from a movie Harold hadn't seen. Whoever was under that great, big cartoon head, smelled like an ashtray, and carried a pack of cigarettes right there in his suit jacket pocket. Pall Malls.

"Time!"

Harold collapsed onto his knees, his shirt sticking to his torso. He got to his feet, used the bottom of his shirt to wipe a bead of sweat off of his temple, and began to gingerly climb into the machine that pulled his legs apart like a wishbone.

"And, begin."

Max and Andy and "Gru" had tried to pretend the guy was just a tall kid, but that seemed unlikely. Who was he? Harold never did find out; the guy hadn't taken off his mask before thanking them for the candy and saying "Happy Halloween" and slipping out the door.

Whoever he was, he'd been the first trick or treater Harold had ever seen who'd scurried back down their walkway, hopped into an old, black-and-white Crown Vic, and driven away. He had, of course, taken his giant cartoon head off to fit in the driver's seat, but the guy had turned his back to Harold, and it was dark.

Harold watched the janitor spray down a neighboring machine. Who was Gru? Could he really be just a kid? Someone Max's age? As far as Harold knew no one at Bridge was that tall.

"Time!" Kate said. "Harold, my dear, come back to me."

A few of the other class members laughed, and Harold realized he'd been sitting in the leg-spreading machine—the *butt-blaster*, he called it—doing nothing. Maybe his glutes needed a rest. He laughed and offered Kate a meek wave of apology.

"Plank position."

Harold looked up at Kate, hoping for mercy, and then at the floor just as those large, yellow and black mountaineering boots sauntered past in front of his nose. The janitor guy stopped at the vacant lat pull-down machine and gave it a spray and a wipe.

"Side planks," Kate said, eliciting more groans. "And, begin."

Harold had considered saying something to "Gru" and/or Max right then and there, but it hadn't seemed appropriate or even all that important at the time, what with his youngest son Gabe reportedly having just spoken. Harold hadn't heard it, nor had Judy, but Max and Andy had been so excited there was little doubt that in this story, at least, they'd told the truth. Gabe had apparently spoken his brother's name. Then he'd gone quiet again.

"Time! Other side!"

Harold's back ached. Temples throbbed. Maybe if he died he would be excused from doing this last set.

"Get those waists in the air!"

Try as he might, Harold couldn't focus. There was, in fact, a lot of drama swirling around Max. It had been a fragile few weeks, with lots of angry phone calls between parents since the poor kid had been voted off the golf team. Harold had lost a great deal of respect for Mr. Raymundo—"Time!"—and he'd never had much respect for Alan Whiting, the top-selling Century 21 agent in Boise, or his oldest son, Peter, the school's best golfer.

Eventually, Max had been invited to reclaim his position as team manager, but Judy had vetoed the idea since it would be, "like returning to an abusive relationship."

Work was another headache. It had been a good fall, with the paper having won a regional journalism award, but the staff's overall morale returned to its usual depths as October gave way to November and rumors swirled that the paper was on the verge of yet more layoffs.

"Next station!"

Harold adjusted the biceps curl machine to fit his six-foot frame.

"And, begin."

Harold tried to lift the handles up toward his nose, but his biceps were shot. He looked down at the pin in the stack of iron, showing he was already on the lowest weight. He was done. He just sat there, not moving, too tired to care if Kate or anyone else made fun of him.

"Time!" She smiled.

"Good work, everybody! You, too, Harold." She winked.

Harold toweled off and stupidly thanked her for another hour of torture before making the slow walk back to the locker room. At least he didn't have to go up any stairs. He was still in the hallway when a poster caught his attention:

"Dig deep and find your best self!"

There was a photo of a snarling slab of muscle clad in what looked to be a velour tracksuit.

Harold smiled.

This, he thought, is exactly what Max needs.

CHAPTER 16

Sadie sat in the driver's seat of a tiny, red econo-box with a really embarrassing decal *Student Driver* on each side, and tried to make sense of the welter of signs up ahead: this way toward Mt. Home, that way toward Nampa, but what about Boise? How come there was no sign for Boise?

Wait—there were two signs for Nampa? What was that about? Which Nampa was the one she wanted? And why wasn't there a sign telling her what to do about Max? And Gabe? And rude Graham Godwin?

"Mt. Home! Mt. Home!" Mr. Ferd said from the front passenger seat.

Sadie swerved across three lanes, barely making it in time. "Sorry!"

The girls in the back shrieked with laughter, but Mr. Ferd was not amused. "Let's think about signaling next time, okay?"

Sadie could feel the disapproval radiating off of not just Mr. F but also from Lilly Robinson and Susannah Jurevicious, who were sitting in the back seat. All they'd had to do was drive through Star, a suburb full of slow-moving cows and even slower moving wheat and barley, while Sadie here was being asked to navigate the only stretch of road in all of Idaho that was like New York City or San Francisco or L.A.

How fair was that?

What was the proper distance at which to follow the car in front of you? She was pretty sure she'd gotten that one right when it was put to her on paper, but here, now, when it mattered and the rubber met the road, Sadie had absolutely no idea. Her mind was mush, her thoughts scattered. She and Graham Godwin were officially finished, done in by—of all things—her turquoise Victoria's Secret purchase, and her refusal to "take it off." Rude. So rude.

Also, there was a lot going on at home, most of it not so good, and on top of everything else, she'd completely forgotten a line and was pretty sure she'd totally muffed her audition for the Bridge Academy secular Christmas play.

"I don't know if I feel safe back here, Mr. F," Lilly said from the back seat. "This car is, like, super tiny and whatever. Can't we get something with a little more metal around it like a Toyota Sequoia or at least a Rav4?"

"Or a Mercedes?" Susannah added. "They're supposed to be pretty safe."

Sadie looked over at Mr. Ferd, who wasn't smiling.

"Eyes on the road," he said. "Just signal next time."

"Point taken, Mr. Ferd," Sadie said, turning hard to the left and easing the car into traffic on Interstate 84. "Sorry about that, everyone, but I felt the situation called for a little quick thinking and evasive—"

"Just signal next time," Mr. Ferd said.

Sadie stole a glance at the rear-view mirror and was pretty sure she caught Susannah smirking, which called for an appropriately icy glare to bounce off the mirror and into the backseat, but Sadie was distracted as their tiny, red car was fast approaching what appeared to be a rectangular house or office suite on a trailer bed.

"Pass on the left," Mr. Ferd said.

Sadie was pretty sure Susannah shouldn't even be here—the girl was only a ninth grader, a year behind Sadie in school, but apparently she was almost 15, or maybe she'd qualified for driver's ed by height. Max's not-so-secret crush had to be at least three inches taller than him. She was even taller than her steady, Peter Whiting. Her *former* steady, if Sadie had heard right.

Rumor had it Susannah had dumped the guy for leading the bloodless coup that stripped Max of his managerial duties with the golf team.

"Take the Broadway exit," Mr. Ferd said.

Sadie had never really understood what Max got out of being manager of the golf team, beyond his two P.E. credits, but she had to agree with Susannah that voting him off the team had been a crappy thing to do. The whole deal had just about crushed her brother's will to live.

"Can we hit the Dutch Brothers drive-through and get a mocha?"

"No, Lilly," Mr. Ferd said, not bothering to look over his shoulder at the two backseat passengers.

"Aw," Lilly and Susannah said in unison.

Sadie turned left on Broadway and pointed the little car toward the foothills, and school. "I respect what you did in the name of my brother," she said, looking over her shoulder at Susannah.

"Eyes on the road," Mr. Ferd said.

"Thanks, I guess," Susannah said. "He sits behind me in Spanish. Figured it was the least I could do, have his back like that, since he has mine. I bummed a pencil off him once. Truth be told Pete and I were near kaput, anyway. Not a happy boy, Pete Whiting. Father issues."

"I'll ask you both to please not distract the driver," Mr. Ferd said.

The light turned green and Sadie eased off the brake pedal.

"You and Graham Godwin went bust, too, no?" Lilly said, as if Mr. Ferd hadn't said anything.

"Lilly," Mr. Ferd said.

Sadie said nothing, but it was true. She couldn't forgive his rudeness, the look in his eyes at the party that night that had told her once and for all what she was to him. There had been a whole spate of breakups at Bridge lately, like they were all part of some weird, pre-Thanksgiving relationship purge. Or maybe it was contagious, or bad luck.

"Graham's not bad looking," Susannah said.

Sadie paid her no mind, the car creeping along through light traffic.

Was it bad luck, all those fall breakups? That seemed possible, given what else had been going down lately. Gabe had gone back to Gabe Land, and Max was moping, and their grim-looking parents were delving into more and more closed conferences in hushed tones. It was like everyone was falling apart at once.

Sadie turned the corner and nosed the econo-box into an open space in front of the school where they all piled out.

Bad luck—maybe that's what it was. At least she hadn't had to parallel park.

CHAPTER 17

Ovals. Gabe looked into the eyes of the brown-haired speech pathologist and saw two ovals, horizontally placed, and then he looked away.

Circles. There were two circles, nostrils, under her nose.

A rectangular sign on the wall, with corresponding pictures: "The quick brown fox jumped over the lazy dog." Six puppets hung from strings attached to the ceiling: a purple unicorn with orange mane; a knight with a red mustache and a suit of armor and shield; a mermaid princess with a yellow crown and pink hair; a wizard whose white hair spilled down over his face; a jester; and a blue-green dragon with a tuft of blond mane.

The room smelled like vanilla. He couldn't tell if that was because speech pathologist Cynthia smelled like vanilla, or if the room just smelled like vanilla. From his spot on the long, brown rectangular couch, he could barely smell his mother, who always smelled like leaves. *Patchouli*, she called her scent. Only she said it, *Patch-oooooooo-li*, smiling as if it was so much fun to say the word. "Like *choo-choo* train," she would add. Max sometimes smelled like Junior Mints, and those were good days because on those occasions, Max was eating Junior Mints, and he always gave some to Gabe.

"Can you say 'truck' Gabe? Can you say it?"

Gabe looked down at the yellow and black toy truck in the hands of speech pathologist Cynthia: four wheels, with four knobby, black tires. *TONKA*, it said on the side, in black letters, all-caps. *Neuro-appropriate responses*—that's what they wanted.

He looked at his mother, sitting in a chair to his left.

"Truck," Cynthia repeated, smiling.

What was she smiling about? He hasn't said a word since they started coming here when he was only nine. Mostly he played with the wood blocks—*manipulatives*, Cynthia called them, when talking to his mom. No one asked him to say *manipulatives*, even though he was sure he could say *manipulatives*. It would be fun to say *manipulatives*.

"Truck," Cynthia said again. "Can you say that, Gabe?"

The blocks were mostly rectangles, but there were also a couple of rhomboids, and some squares, and a bridge-shaped thing, which was really just a rectangle with a half a circle drilled out the bottom of it. And there were the five parallelograms, Gabe's favorite. He liked the way you could lay them down horizontally and they seemed to point down the straightaway. They looked fast.

"Truck," his mom said. "Can you say that, honey?"

His eyes roamed. A rectangular sign on the wall: "The rain in Spain falls mainly on the plains." Cynthia's desk was a rectangle. The room was a square. The ceiling had square tiles with holes in them, 14 across and 14 down, 196 holes in total. The blocks were kept in a wicker basket—rectangular—in an open shelving unit behind where his mom was sitting.

"Truck?" Cynthia was moving the little toy car across the top of her desk now, making her lips blubber together quickly. Truck noises—she thought she was making truck noises.

"T-t-t-t-t-t-t," Cynthia said, "r-r-r-r-r-r," but he couldn't hear her so well anymore as his mind had moved on to other things. The sound of her voice had faded, like she was under a burlap bag.

The office building that they sat in was just across I-84 from the airport, which was full of airplanes, cylindrical tubes with rhombus wings and rhombus tails and cylindrical engines attached to those rhombus wings and sometimes on either side of the rhombus tails and a bunch of retractable round tires—eight? 16?—down below.

The office had a vertical-horizontal door, the building had a vertical-horizontal door, his mom's chair had four legs, his tongue tasted like peanut butter crackers, he heard a siren wailing in the distance. He hummed and rocked in his seat.

"We'll try again next week," his mom said, standing.

"What does he *like*?" Cynthia was standing, too, brushing something off the blue skirt that came down over her thighs.

Shapes, Gabe thought. *I like shapes.*

"Star Wars," his mom said. She turned to face him now. "Isn't that right, Gabe? Whew! So frustrating! But we'll try again next time, won't we, Gabe?"

But he was hardly listening now, his mind having locked onto the image in his head of the Star Wars TIE Fighter with its spherical, orb-like cockpit and six-sided wings. Hexagon. *Hexagonal.*

"Star Wars, then," Cynthia said, turning to Gabe. "Next week we're going to a land far, far away. Right, Gabe?"

Gabe heard a ripping noise and looked down to find his mother was zipping up his parka.

"And with any luck," his mother said, "we'll bring him back."

His mother shook Cynthia's hand. "Thanks, as always." Gabe felt a little pat on his back, right between his shoulder blades. "C'mon, Gabe, we need to get home and start the turkey. We've got a special guest this year!"

CHAPTER 18

Max's father sat at the head of the table, the end of the table closest to the front of the house. His mother sat at the other end, the one closest to the kitchen. Max sat to the right of Sadie and directly across from Gabe, who sat next to Dewey Tomlinson—the 2014 Buras Family Thanksgiving Guest. Well, Max thought, at least it won't be boring.

How Dewey had wound up there was initially a little surprising to Max, given the lengths he'd gone to in order to keep his new friendship "on the down low," but on second thought going public had only been a matter of time. Max was a notoriously terrible liar and his father was part bloodhound, so it shouldn't have been so surprising when he called a "family meeting," which Max and Sadie knew meant business.

"Your mother and I have been talking," their dad started out.

They were in the living room, the three kids on the couch—the same one where Dewey had left his Pall Malls—and their parents on the love seat.

"Yeah?" Max said.

"Yeah," his father said.

Max hoped he was misreading the grim determination on his dad's face. He tried to stay cool. "What about?"

"The good news is you're not grounded anymore," his father said.

"Oh!" Max said. "I mean, great! Thanks!"

"The bad news is we're going to need to know who 'Gru' is," his father said. "And keep in mind, we're going to need you to come clean this time, or you'll look back fondly at the time you were grounded for only three weeks."

"Honey, we just want to hear the truth," his mother said. "We won't be mad. We know he's not just some kid from the neighborhood."

"We know he's an adult," his father said. "We saw him drive away."

"Duh," Sadie said. "You guys are just figuring that out now?"

"Sadie!" their mother said.

"We've known for a while now." Dad now. "We just haven't brought it up because—well, it was a question of timing. Max, we knew you were still processing the business with Peter Whiting and so forth, and his father, and we knew how hard that was, so in the interest of not piling on, we held off until now."

Realizing he was out of options, Max told the straight truth. He told them how Dewey had shown up one day, out of the blue, with the tow truck. He told them how he said he was from Oregon, and how he claimed to be Judy Buras's cousin, and how Max remembered that they'd visited that one time in Pendleton, Oregon.

"Oh, my," Max's mom had said then. "The black sheep. He just showed up at our doorstep? But you barely know each other. And now you two are... friends?"

Max told them how a psychic medium had told Dewey to be on high alert for "a talisman," and how he, Dewey, hadn't even known what a talisman was, and how he'd come to the realization that Max was his so-called talisman, or lucky charm, or whatever. Max explained how Max was lucky for Dewey, and Dewey was lucky for Max, and how Dewey had won at video poker, and how he, Max, had won 718 M&M's.

His father got the little wrinkle he sometimes got above his nose.

"So—where does he live again?"

"The Grandview Motel," Max said. "He started out at the Red Lion down by the river, but he moved."

His mother tousled her hair and forced a smile. "And what happened to the tow truck?"

"He had to give it back," Max said. "He bought an old police cruiser."

"Yeah," his father said. "I saw that, on Halloween night."

Sadie, sitting next to Max in the couch, said nothing. She checked her watch.

"So that's pretty much everything," Max said. "I guess I didn't want to tell you because I thought you wouldn't understand. I thought you'd think it was weird, or he was weird, or I was in danger, which I wasn't. I'm not—in danger, that is. Dewey's good company, despite the smoking."

"Oh, honey, we don't think it's weird at all," his mother said. "Right Harold? We don't think it's weird, do we? It's perfectly normal to have friends, and some of them are going to be just like us, and others—"

"I think it's weird," his father said. "How old is this guy?"

"I'm not 100 percent sure," Max said, deciding to leave out the fact that Dewey wasn't sure, either.

"Weird," Max's father said again.

"Oh, Harold," Max's mother said. "It's *perfectly* normal!" She was smiling and looking at Max and Sadie for backup.

"He's ancient," Sadie said. "You should have seen his comb-over, before he got it all cut off. It was atrocious."

"He's self-conscious about his teeth," Max said.

"Well, I can't think of one reason why we shouldn't invite him over for Thanksgiving," his mother said. "Let's get to know Dewey Tomlinson! Uncle Dewey!"

✿ ✿ ✿

Max looked down at his heaping dinner. Sadie helped herself to the giant bowl of sweet potato tots, while their mother buttered her roll. Max's father ladled up a scoop of cranberry sauce and plopped it onto his plate, next to a few thick slabs of turkey.

"Max," his mother said. "Would you say the blessing?"

They held hands around the table, except for Gabe, Max assumed, since his brother was not big into the hand-holding. Max bowed his head and closed his eyes, but something compelled him to peek across the table. He was only half right—Gabe's left arm hung straight down, far from their father, but Gabe's right hand lay flat, palm-down, atop Dewey's left, which rested on the white tablecloth.

"Heavenly Father known by many names," Max began, "thank you for bringing us together on this occasion, and for the food on our plates and the roof over our heads, and for my brother Gabe and also for Uncle Dewey here and, um, my sister Sadie. And my mom and dad, too, and Mars, even though he's shaped like a furry toaster—amen."

"Amen," his mother said. "Eat up, everybody! Happy Thanksgiving!"

"Sure is good of you to have me," Dewey said. The pile of food on his plate hit just about every color in the crayon box: orange, green, red, white.

"Glad you could come," Max's father said. "You work at the Y, right?"

"Sure do indeed. Been there only a couple weeks. Janitorial. I needed a job once I blew in from Pendleton." Dewey winked across the table at Max.

"Right. I thought I recognized you. I take a class over there, it meets three times a week, but I usually make only one or two. Stride, it's called, a real ball-buster, or maybe the teacher just is."

"Harold," Max's mother said.

Dewey laughed. "But that's the point, ain't it?"

"I suppose you're right." Max's father used his fork to gesture toward his heaping plate of food. "I guess it's how I can justify this. I'm not gonna lie, it's a little more work when you get older. I'm not 25 anymore."

"We know," Sadie said.

Max had never heard his father talk quite like this—more like a trucker than an educated newspaperman.

Gabe kept gaping at the guy seated to his right, like Dewey was a long-lost relative or something. Max was pretty sure he'd caught his brother smiling, which was rare. Gabe gazed over Max's left shoulder at the framed print Dewey had bought at Ross Dress For Less. The print was just a bunch of rectangles and one or two squares, basically, but Max's parents had made a big fuss of thanks and propped it up on the kitchen counter. And if Gabe liked it, Max decided, then whoever made the print was Max's new favorite artist.

His parents interrogated Dewey even while making it sound as if they were just making polite conversation. Max had to hand it to them—they were good. Maybe it was his father's journalism training.

Dewey explained how he'd been raised in foster homes around the Pacific Northwest, how he'd dropped out of school and begun "a life in the trades," and how this had entailed a checkered work history. There were some gaps in the story, but his parents didn't point them out, and when Dewey got up to go outside and have a smoke, it didn't look as if he did so out of the need to take evasive action.

"He's a nice man," Max's mother said.

"Tall," Max's father said. "Big feet. Big boots."

"He bought them at the mall," Sadie said.

"What?" their mother said.

Sadie finished chewing. "Never mind," she said

Dewey came back in, and everyone went for seconds.

"The turkey is perfect," Dewey said. "It's not overcooked."

"You're nice to say so," Max's mother said. "I think it's a bit dry, but that's what the gravy is for." She laughed and poured some on her plate.

Dewey worked some more food down his throat. "Oh, for sure, that is some good gravy, Mrs. B, the real deal. And the sweet potatoes—mmmm, mmm!"

Dewey turned to his right. "Isn't that right, Gabe?"

"Mmmm, mmm," someone repeated.

Max looked up from his turkey.

"Mmmm, mmm."

This time there was no doubt as to which of them had said it: Gabe.

Max looked over at his mother, whose hand, loaded up with a buttered roll, had frozen a few inches in front of her mouth.

"Truck," Gabe said.

The buttered roll fell out of her hand, hit the edge of a plate, and fell off the table and hit the floor. She made no move to pick it up and Mars immediately moved in and began licking it.

"Truck," Gabe said again. Mars's tags jangled as he worked his little jaws.

"Oh. My. God." Sadie looked at their mother. "Mom?"

"You like trucks, buddy?" Dewey stabbed a piece of turkey with his fork and swirled it around in some gravy. "Wish I still had the tow, I bet—"

"Dad," Sadie said. "Are you hearing this?"

Max worked a mouthful of turkey down his throat so he could breathe again.

"Truck," Gabe said again.

"Truck," their mother finally croaked. "Good, Gabe. Truck."

"Yes!" their father said. "Truck! Truck! Truck!"

He laughed.

Gabe looked at Max.

"Max," Gabe said.

He had tucked into a sort of crouch in his chair, his hands on an imaginary steering wheel, his body tilting left and right as if he was flying through space.

"Hex," he said. "Hexagon. Hexagon. *Hexagonal.*"

Max recognized it immediately: His brother wasn't in Gabe Land, he was in Star Wars land.

"The TIE fighter," Max said. "Hexagonal."

Gabe stopped with the imaginary flying and looked down at his food, and then across the table at his older brother.

"Yeah," he said.

❈ ❈ ❈

Gabe lay asleep by the fire, no doubt tired out from speaking more at dinner than he had for his first 10 years. Only his head was visible; a Star Wars sleeping bag covered the rest of him. Uncle Dewey's gift, the framed print with all of its rectangles and squares, lay flat at Gabe's side.

Max's parents were cleaning up in the kitchen, and doing a lot of whispering and, every time Max looked up from the living room couch, smiling at each other like they'd just met.

"Dewey wants to watch the Cowboys game," Max hollered from the couch. "That okay?"

"Sure, honey." His mom handed his dad a large, green platter, which he began to dry with a blue dishrag.

"Let me know who's winning," she said.

"Okay, we'll be in here if you need us," Max said. He and Dewey made their way into the TV room, closed the door and found the game on TV.

"Great night," Dewey said. "Oh! Cowboys are up a touchdown."

Max let his eyes settle on the cheerleaders, who seemed to get as much airtime as the game itself.

"You're a Cowboys fan? I figured you for a Seattle Seahawks fan, like everyone else around here."

"They're America's Team—Cowboys fans are everywhere." Dewey reached into his jeans pocket and produced a toothpick, which he inserted into his mouth. "Toothpick?"

"Nah," Max said. "I'm good."

"Cigarette?" Dewey said. "Just kidding. So you're brother talks. I didn't know he didn't, before."

"No, he didn't," Max said. "He was quiet as a mouse."

"Huh," Dewey said.

"Yeah, huh," Max repeated.

Dewey pried something out of his teeth and looked down at the toothpick. "Sorry about the thing with the golf team. Your dad said you were pretty upset. It true you didn't get out of bed for two days?"

"Yeah. Well, I mean, I used the bathroom, if that counts."

Dewey laughed. "No. Using the bathroom doesn't count. I'm counting that as two days in bed. Don't worry about those guys."

"The thing that hurt the most was Mr. Raymundo," Max said. "I guess I thought he'd stick up for me or something, but he just—he just rolled over. Now they want to get rid of him; that's what my dad said, anyway. He talked to the principal. It's become a whole big *thing*."

Dewey turned away from the TV set. "So why don't they? If they want to get rid of him, why don't they just get rid of him? It isn't that hard. Not like he can't be replaced."

Max shrugged. "I guess no one else at the school plays golf—not even badly, like Mr. Raymundo."

"I play golf." Dewey smiled at Max, as if he knew this would provoke more than a modicum of surprise.

"You do?"

"Don't act so surprised." Dewey laughed. "I had a foster family that was into it when I was 11—the dad, especially. He got me lessons. I got pretty okay at it, actually. You should try it—it's not that hard." He turned back to the football game. "Anyway," he added. "Don't worry about those guys. That never should've happened."

The game went to commercial, and Max aimed the remote and muted the sound as Dewey turned on the couch to face him. "So no more being grounded.

We gotta get out there again, no? Get some of that bio-harmonic convergence going again? Replenish the coffers? I don't see myself cleaning the johns at the YMCA when I'm 50."

"You don't like it?"

"I like it fine," Dewey said. "I just don't think it's much of a long-term career, or if it is, it's not exactly the long-term career I had in mind."

"What is?"

"I don't know, exactly." Dewey looked at his wrist as if the cheap digital watch might hold the answer. "Mountaineering?"

On TV the Dallas cheerleaders were smiling and kicking up their legs, and Max turned the sound back on as Dewey flashed him a sly smile. "You got a girlfriend?"

The look on his face was contagious, and Max found himself smiling that way, too. "Nah," he said as if he was just too busy, or he had simply chosen to be lonely all the time.

Dewey was still smiling. "Got your eye on anyone?"

"Sort of." Max looked at his feet.

"Ah, ha! The truth comes out!" Dewey said. "So ask her out! C'mon! You're a good-lookin' dude! She'd be crazy not to say yes."

"So, mountaineering," Max said.

"Mountaineering?"

"There could be money in that," Max said, wondering if it was true. Dewey could always be counted on to be interested in money.

Dewey said nothing, so Max continued before the conversation could veer back to girlfriends again. "Do you ever have doubts? About us, I mean, and this whole bio-harmonic convergence thing? I don't know about you, but for me the luck seems to fade in and out. I have my good days and my bad days, and getting voted off the golf team didn't seem lucky."

Dewey nodded, as if he expected this might come up. "You gotta keep in mind, we hadn't seen each other for a while. The magic had rubbed off. I couldn't even win a hand on the machine at Emerald Lanes, which is the loosest video poker machine in the entire Treasure Valley."

"I guess so," Max said, muting the TV again as the game went to commercials.

"I forgot to tell you," Dewey said, "I found out my birthday, like you asked me to—my *real* birthday, not the date they stamped on my driver's license when I said I didn't know it. I had to call all over the damn place, but I found out.

"And I think that explains it, just like you predicted," Dewey added. "You know we share a birthday with George Lucas and Rob Gronkowski?"

"Who's Rob Gronkowski?"

"Football player."

"Does he play for the Cowboys?"

"No. It doesn't matter. The point is, I found a book, Max."

Max turned to face Dewey. "What kind of book?"

"It's a birthday book. It's about, like, numerology and astrology and, you know, birthdays. You look up the day you were born, it tells you all sorts of stuff. You and me, our birthday, we got some challenges ahead of us, brother."

Max's ears perked up. Maybe this would explain his problems with his eyesight, and the golf team, and Susannah Jurevicious. "Challenges?"

"What we're dealing with," Dewey said, "according to the book, is a quote-unquote *ongoing battle to maintain stability.* So that's the bad news. But hang on a sec."

Dewey reached into his pocket, the same one that held the toothpicks, and produced a sheaf of YMCA stationery folded into eighths or sixteenths.

"I wrote the rest of this down so I'd get it right."

He looked down at the piece of paper and began to read: "The best way for those born on this day to mitigate against such aforementioned instability…"

"What's mitigate mean?" Max interrupted.

Dewey looked up from his piece of paper. "To, I don't know, *counteract* something," he said. He looked back down at his writing: "The way to counteract the instability is to ally themselves with—join *forces* with—*others also born on this day.* In fact, the planets suggest such joining of forces may lead to a *powerful alchemy.*"

He looked up.

"Powerful alchemy!" Dewey said again.

"Whoa," Max said. "Alchemy—magic!"

"Yep," Dewey said. "I looked it up in the dictionary, just to be sure."

"It says all that about March 7?"

Dewey shot up out of the couch as if he'd sat on a pin. "What?"

"March 7th," Max said again. The football game had come back on the TV, behind Dewey, and the cheerleaders were on again.

"That's your birthday?" Dewey said. "March 7th?"

"Yeah—March 7th, 2001. Why? What's yours?"

Dewey's shoulders slumped; he looked a good six inches shorter than he had just 30 seconds ago. "May 14th," he said. "I thought we—"

"Hang on," Max said, getting to his feet.

He opened the TV room door and slipped out into the dining room, careful not to slam it closed so as not to disturb the sleeping Gabe in the next room. Only their mom was still in the kitchen, cleaning up.

"Hi, Mom."

"Oh, hi, honey."

Max looked over at the whirring dishwasher. "I should know this, but when is Gabe's birthday?"

His mother was drying the salad bowl. "Oh, it's not for a while, honey. Did you see something he'd like? You could always get it for him for Christmas. I'm sure he'd love it."

"No, it's not that." Max looked over at the pile of clean dishes next to the sink. "It's just—when's his birthday?" He'd never had much of a head for numbers, other than the M&M's thing, and he focused hard so as not to forget what Dewey had said. *Ongoing battle to maintain stability. Bio-harmonic convergence. Powerful alchemy. May 14th.*

Max's mother put the salad bowl down.

"Well," she said, "Gabe was born on May 14th."

CHAPTER 19

The next few months brought sweeping changes.

After an initial twinge of disappointment at not being the chosen one, and not being in "bio-harmonic convergence" with Dewey, Max felt somewhat relieved to know he would no longer be spending time at the tall man's side as he played video poker. Not that they'd done that for a while. What's more, he was happy for Gabe that something was finally going right in his life, even if it was something weird.

It was December 18, the first day of Christmas break, and this meant, among other things, so many people would be heading out of town that much of Boise would all but shut down. Max and Andy would get a reprieve from grunting and sweating and throwing medicine balls around the Boise High gymnasium with Boise High Braves hammer throw coach, Rock Bromley, barking in their ears, (Max's father's wonderful idea).

Max stood in front of the bathroom mirror and looked at his torso, which was so white and fleshy as to resemble the underside of a trout. No part of him seemed bigger, firmer, or stronger. His arms and shoulders hurt, his lower back ached, and he'd broken the nail on his right index finger, but that was all he had to show for three weeks of Rock Bromley's Hammer Throw Boot Camp.

"What are we doing here?" Andy had asked at their first class.

"Penance," Max said.

Max's dad had seen it posted outside the locker room at the Y and had picked up a flier. It had a photo of Rock Bromley in all of his bull-necked, unnaturally tanned glory, a muscular gift to the hammer throw wrapped in a shiny, maroon tracksuit and with a buzz-cut, blond-frosted hairdo.

"You're going," his dad said, dropping the flier in front of Max as he ate his after-school bowl of cereal, and Max knew better than to argue.

As he stood there in front of the mirror, Max had the sneaking suspicion his dad was having way too much fun with this. Max raised his arms up above his head, still eying his spongy form. He dropped his hands, raised them again. Wait. Were those pecs? Or were those man-boobs?

Ivor Jenks, two-time high school state champion and star of the Rock Bromley Hammer Throw Boot Camp, would have called them man-boobs. Max wondered what Tiffany Briggs, Bromley's other favorite, would have called them. Andy, who had been a good sport to join Max amid the other campers, didn't have much in the way of muscles, either. The poor guy had been so sore after the first session he hadn't been able to lift his arms above his head, and Max had had to help his friend get a dry shirt over his shoulders in the locker room.

"Max! I need the bathroom! I need to get ready!" Sadie screamed as Max looked first at his watch, then at the closed bathroom door.

"Just a minute!" He looked around the bathroom for his red and yellow striped shirt, which he found crumpled in a ball on the floor. "Just give me a minute, okay? Trust me, you're not going to want to rush in here."

"Ew, gross! Mom!"

"Mom's not here."

"I'm telling Mom."

"Telling her what?"

"I don't know. I'll think of something. What are you doing? Gawd, don't answer that. You've been in there for like a week and a half!"

"Calm down," Max said, opening the door to find Sadie in pajamas with her hair up. "Geez, Sade, such drama! Save it for the stage, why don't you."

"You save it for the stage," she said. "I've got to get ready."

Max heard her shut the door and walked up the hallway toward the kitchen. He looked through the window at Mars, who was stalking a chipmunk in the backyard. Max lifted his arms over his head again, feeling the soreness from his unusually active last three weeks, a good soreness. If they weren't pecs, well then his pecs were in there somewhere.

He walked to the YMCA to find them, with or without Rock Bromley.

CHAPTER 20

"Truck." Speech pathologist Cynthia rolled a Tonka truck on her desk.

"Truck," Gabe said from his spot on the couch across from her. He looked down at the tiny, die-cast "TIE fighter" with the hexagonal wings in his fingers—his *fidget toy*, Max had called it, upon gifting it to his brother. Dewey smiled at the term.

"Good, Gabe!" Cynthia smiled. "Train. Can you say train, Gabe?"

"Train."

"Good!"

Selective mutism—that was the official diagnosis, now that Gabe was talking, sometimes as if he'd never had a problem at all. Dewey had never heard of such a condition, but according to the American Academy of Child and Adolescent Psychiatry it affected roughly seven of every 1,000 kids, and it was rooted in nerves and social anxiety disorder, which explained why, other than those one or two times he'd said stuff around the house, Gabe didn't talk. Only now, with Dewey having come into their lives, Gabe seemed to feel more at ease, and this newfound sense of calm had compelled him to start using his vocal chords.

"Train," Gabe said again.

The room smelled like vanilla air freshener, diplomas dotted the wall, and a glass vase of rather tired looking flowers occupied the desk next to the room's lone window. Cynthia and Gabe sat opposite one another, Cynthia at her tidy desk and Gabe sunken into the big, brown puffy couch. Gabe's mother sat well behind Gabe.

The satisfied smile on Judy Buras's face gave way to a quizzical expression as she appraised Gabe's "talk doc," as Harold called her.

"You look different!" Judy said. "Did you just get off a tropical vacation? Did you get your hair done differently?"

Cynthia smiled, her color flashing slightly redder in the cheeks and neck. "No, it's the same old me. But thanks!"

Judy pressed on. "Did you start working out? I mean, not that you *needed* to lose any weight, heavens no. You just look so—"

Cynthia looked up again and smiled. "It's the same old me!"

"Well, you don't look old," Judy said. "You look absolutely radiant!"

"Thank you," Cynthia said.

"Radiant," Gabe said.

"Yes! Radiant!" Dewey Tomlinson said, since everyone else was saying it.

He was normally not quite so free with a compliment, and never would have come up with the word himself—*radiant!*—but such was his new role as Gabe's paid driver and friend, Mrs. Buras's hired nanny, of sorts, that Dewey had recently found himself doing a lot of new things. Like speech therapy, for one thing. Mrs. Buras had insisted that his presence there was "non-negotiable." In Dewey's presence, Gabe spoke.

From his vantage point, sitting in a too-small, camel-colored chair that swiveled, next to his new employer, Mrs. Buras, Dewey had come to the conclusion that speech pathologist Cynthia wasn't exactly terrible looking. If radiant was the word for it, then so be it, she was radiant. He'd have said she was a babe. She had dark hair, pulled back and tied off to form a longish ponytail, and striking blue-gray eyes and an ivory complexion and pinkish cheeks. Dewey reflexively reached over his head to finger-comb his dirty-blond hair, but then remembered he no longer had it—he'd gotten it all cut off.

"My goodness!" Cynthia said, blushing. "Thank you, all!"

"You're welcome," Dewey said.

Gabe smiled at him and held up the miniature Star Wars fighter plane, and Dewey held his gaze for a quick second as he held up his own Star Wars TIE fighter, an exact replica of Gabe's.

After all of the astonishment and tears and explanations and slapdash experiments meant to take Dewey and Gabe's newly discovered "bio-harmonic convergence" out for a spin Thanksgiving night, Max had, on Black Friday, made his way to Boise Book and Game and purchased the two identical die-cast TIE fighters.

Dewey's TIE fighter didn't really fit in his pocket, as the hexagonal wings were only a little smaller than the top of a tuna fish can, but Gabe rarely parted with his. They were meant to remind each of them of the other, that was the idea, Max said. Mrs. B said they were like "long-lost friends, reunited."

Until the last three weeks Dewey had noticed a growing heaviness about Mrs. Buras—not literally, but a world-weariness that no doubt came of all those fruitless attempts to rally Gabe to come to his senses and join the party. That weariness was gone now. Despite his quick assent ("Yes! Radiant!") Dewey knew nothing of Cynthia's improved appearance, or even if indeed she did look better than before. Until three weeks ago he'd never met her; he wouldn't have known. But it was easy to explain the recent transformation in Mrs. Buras. There could be little doubt Gabe's dramatic improvement had been responsible for her elevated mood and improved appearance, the color in her cheeks, the increased frequency of her smiles.

Dewey was looking less and less like himself, too, which he conceded might not be such a terrible thing. The trials of his 33 years had left their mark, but in the 21 days since Thanksgiving, which he'd spent working part-time for the Burases and part-time at the Y, he'd put on 101 pounds. He'd noticed a crescent-shaped, milky-white paunch forming under his belly button. He'd even noticed his face filling out some, all of which he attributed to Mrs. B's cooking, which was prolific and delicious and was about to hit another high point. Dewey had been invited to celebrate Christmas with the family, just like Thanksgiving.

"Radiant," Gabe said again.

"Well, my goodness," Cynthia said. "I'm afraid all of this flattery has gotten me a little flustered. Where was I?" She tousled her bangs out of her face and consulted a small notepad on her desk. She stole a glance at Dewey, quickening his pulse, and looked back down at her desk.

"Ah, yes, here we go. The trains. The trains."

"Say, what's that on your desk there? Next to your notepad?" Dewey pointed to what from all appearances looked like 16 ounces of toxic sludge with a lid and a straw.

"It's a green drink," Cynthia said. "It's got kale, beets, carrots—"

"You mean like a salad in a cup?"

She smiled at him. "Yes, you could say that, although I never thought of it that way. It's a smoothie, sort of. I'm not 19 anymore. You have—"

She held him in her gaze, and Dewey felt his heartbeat in his temples.

"You have a way with words," she said.

Dewey smiled. "A regular Hemingway, I am."

Cynthia laughed. Mrs. Buras cleared her throat. "Shall we continue?"

Dewey's first impression of Cynthia had been that she was older than he was, but now he began to wonder if she wasn't younger. He wondered if she would ever go for a guy like him. Nah. Probably not—I mean look at her, she was way out of his league.

They were both getting paid to be here, so they had that in common, at least. That was something. Although Dewey suspected Cynthia was making more than 10 bucks an hour, roughly 20 hours a week, that he'd worked out with Mr. and Mrs. Buras since the "miracle"—Mrs. Buras's word—at Thanksgiving.

It was a strange job, getting paid to hang out with Gabe, but Mr. and Mrs. Buras were of the opinion that after 10 years of running into "developmental dead ends"—Mr. Buras's words—you didn't question it when your kid suddenly started talking, when the doctors took scary words like *Asperger* and *autism* off the table and replaced them with the totally made-up sounding *selective mutism*. You just went with it. You hired the guy who seemed to bring the talk out of the kid, even if that guy was Dewey, the black sheep, the one who made poor choices and wound up in the joint. If Mrs. B knew about that, well, she was too nice to say so, and Dewey certainly wasn't about to bring it up.

"The passengers got off the bus at the station," Cynthia said.

"The passengers...got the bus station." Gabe smacked his legs with both hands, so hard it must have stung a little. Dewey cringed.

"No, that's wonderful!" Cynthia said, writing something in her notepad. "I'm encouraged and you should be, too! I can see we've been practicing!"

"Oh, we've been doing more than that," Judy Buras said with a wink, nodding at Dewey to her right.

With two part-time jobs and his new role as Gabe's muse, Dewey had more responsibility than ever. He gave a meek smile, or as much of a smile as he could while pressing his lips together. He cursed his rotten teeth, crossed his right leg over his left and studied the airy pockets of his brown cargo pants, the black and yellow laces of his mountaineering boots.

"The passengers got off the bus at the station," Gabe said. No breaks. No hesitation. He smiled broadly at Dewey, raised his tie fighter into the air, and brought his legs up into the couch to sit Indian style.

"Yeah," Gabe added. "The passengers at the station."

"Spectacular!" Cynthia said.

"Oh, honey," Mrs. Buras said, but tears had welled up in her eyes and she reached for a Kleenex.

She blew her nose, a wet, juicy honk. "Oh, my goodness. Excuse me."

"The quick brown fox jumped over the lazy dog," Cynthia said.

"The quick brown fox...jumped over...the dog."

"L-a-z-y," Cynthia said.

"Tired," Gabe said.

He leaned back into the couch cushions and smiled at Dewey as Cynthia and Mrs. B squealed with delight. Dewey had to hand it to the kid: He was doing well for someone who supposedly had been locked away in a silent prison for much of his childhood.

"The rain in Spain falls mainly on the plains," Cynthia said.

"The rain in Spain...fills up plains." Gabe smiled and scratched something behind his ear.

"Good!"

Gabe looked out the window at the parking lot. Cynthia pushed back from her desk and stood to her full height, around five feet, seven inches, if Dewey had his weights and measures right—it was a nice height. She approached the open shelving at the wall and scooped up a stack of large flashcards, each about the size and shape of a child's lunch box and each one showing a human face in various emotional states.

Card.

"Happy," Gabe said.

"Good!" Cynthia cooed.

Card.

"Sad," Gabe said.

"Good!"

Card.

"That's frightened or alarmed," Cynthia said. She looked at Mrs. Buras. "I am going to say, based on our rate of progress, those will come with time. With full-blown autism or even with Asperger's he'd have had far more trouble with these."

"Could it be confused?" Dewey said, referencing the card that had stumped Gabe.

No one said anything, and Dewey, embarrassed, thought about his lousy teeth. If only he was getting paid enough to buy new ones, or even enough to go mountaineering, which he'd read about on the computers with the free Internet at the Boise library.

If only he had enough money, then he would lace up his boots, throw a rope over his shoulder, take Cynthia by the hand, and climb into the clouds amid the Grand Tetons. They were only six hours away, by car. Maybe they could make a weekend of it.

"*I* think he looks frightened or alarmed," Mrs. B said. She turned to Dewey. "But I can also see confused." She threw him a wink and stood up. "Cynthia, I'm afraid we've got to go. It's almost show time! Are you sure you can't use the ticket to the Bridge Christmas play? It's totally secular! And now sugar-free!" She laughed.

"Oh, I'm afraid not," Cynthia said. Dewey's heart sank. "But thanks for the offer. Tell Sadie I said hello, and I'm sure she's going to knock it out of the park."

Dewey unfolded from the chair, and tucked his shirt back into the back of his pants as they all made their way for the exit. For some reason he looked over his shoulder at the glass vase on Cynthia's desk, but the arrangement of white, yellow and lavender had been transformed, or his vision had been transformed, or something. The flowers didn't look new again, but they were no longer drawn-out and half-dead, either. It was as if speech therapy, and all this talk of the truck and the train, the quick fox and the rain in Spain, had left them all reinvigorated—even the flowers.

✿ ✿ ✿

All in all it was a strange but good time to be Dewey Tomlinson. First a psychic had told him his lucky charm was on its way to him, and then it was there, right in front of him until, come to find out at Thanksgiving, it was really Max's little brother all along.

On the one hand it all made perfect sense: No one had faced more of an *ongoing battle to maintain stability* than Gabe and Dewey. Still, the news came as a shock.

"I don't get it," Dewey told Max that night in front of the Buras's modest flat screen TV. Max had turned it off in order to deliver the bio-harmonic surprise that Dewey was simpatico with Gabe, not Max, as they'd believed for nearly three months.

Max adjusted his glasses. "What don't you get?"

"How is it he's the one, Gabe is the one, when you've been my wing man all this time? It's the two of us that have been hanging out, not me and Gabe."

"True," Max said, "But the two times you and Gabe *have* hung out have led to magic. *Alchemy*. And isn't that what your book predicted?"

"Are you telling me Max Buras and Dewey Tomlinson haven't been magic? Because I don't know if I believe that."

"You said yourself I wasn't a guarantee," Max said. "You lost, too. I saw you lose. How much did you really win on those machines, anyway?"

Dewey knew Max had a point. He hadn't won all that much, really. He was nowhere near rich enough to get new teeth. He'd had to get a job, at the Y.

"But why were YOU lucky, Max?"

"I told you I had doubts, didn't I? Just now. We were sitting right here watching the game. I said I didn't feel all that lucky a lot of the time."

"Aw," Dewey said, "I just figured you were sore about the golf team thing and Mr. Raymundo and Peter Whiting. Didn't you say you made everyone but Whiting lucky that one day? The day, like, I think it was maybe a month before the district tournament?"

"That could have been anything," Max said. "A bad day—even the great

Pete Whiting has those. He's had two I can think of, just off the top of my head."

"Boy, he sure had one at districts," Dewey said.

"So did Mr. Raymundo," Max said. "I still can't believe he didn't—"

"Wait! Answer me this: What about the M&M's?" Dewey smiled, revealing his crazy lineup of creamed-corn teeth.

"That," Max said, "I have no answer for." Pause. "There is one explanation."

"Yeah?"

"Let's say you were lucky," Max said. "I don't know if we'll ever know one way or the other, but let's just say for the sake of argument."

"Okay."

Max smiled. "Have you ever had a dog?"

"I've been around some foster families that had 'em."

"So you know how when you go out in public, sometimes another dog will sniff your leg or your foot or something? And the owner will say, 'Do you have a dog?' And you'll say, 'Yes, his name is Mars.' And the owner of the other dog will say, looking at his dog, 'He must smell your dog.'"

Dewey looked down at the couch, across at the TV, and up at Max. "So you're saying—"

"I'm saying maybe I had Gabe on me when I left the house," Max said. "And the Gabe and the *alchemy* got on you, Dewey, and you, Dewey, got lucky."

Dewey laughed. "The Gabe got on you and then it got on me? I don't know if I'm quite with you there. Nice idea, though."

"Yeah," Max said. "It sounded better before I said it aloud. I have no explanation for any of it."

CHAPTER TWENTY ONE

CHAPTER

Winter break flew by in no time, as it always did. Dewey, of course, celebrated Christmas with the family, and his presence not only brought the words spilling out of Gabe, as usual, it seemed to green the needles on the Buras family tree.

"Mom, why does Dewey make Gabe more like normal?" Max asked that night, when Dewey had gone back to the Grandview Motel and Gabe had gone to bed.

"We don't know that, honey. And, well, your father and I, we're curious, too, but…"

"But what?"

"Well, I guess we didn't want to jinx it," his mother said. She laughed. "That sounds silly, but there you go. We don't understand it, we don't, but we're not sure we *have* to understand it. We're just grateful, honey. We're very, very grateful for Uncle Dewey."

"Sure," Max said. "Me, too."

He was wearing a new sweater, part of his big Christmas present: new clothes from his parents "to "accommodate all those new muscles," was how his dad put it. Max wasn't sure how much his physique had really changed, but he appreciated the thought. His other big Christmas present was a golf instructional DVD with the long and unwieldy name of, "SyberVision Men's Muscle Memory Programming for Golf with Al Geiberger."

"Found it for three bucks at a yard sale," Dewey said.

"Dewey!" Sadie said. "You're not supposed to say the price."

"Well, I spent 20 more getting it converted from VHS to DVD!" Dewey said. "If that counts for anything."

"Cool," Max said, wondering if it really was.

"It's not how I learned," Dewey said. "But I always regretted that I didn't—too many bad habits. Gotta start right early! That's how the pros all got going, they were young."

Sadie did just fine in Bridge Academy's secular production of *The Elves and the Shoemaker*. She remembered all her lines. Hadley Jackson, one of the two golfers who had stuck up for Max as he'd been voted off the team, played the male lead, Lilly Robinson the female lead.

Poor Mrs. Hickenlooper, who taught drama in addition to math, had thought it would be a good idea to recruit the kids from nearby Giraffe Laugh Preschool to play the elves, since they were so small, but getting them to stand and deliver their lines on cue had been like herding cats.

Mr. Raymundo would no longer be the golf coach when they came back from break, which wouldn't matter for a few months, until spring. He also had been dealt a one-month suspension from teaching Spanish, which mostly coincided with winter break and which necessitated a few classes with a sub named Mr. Hoover, whom Max wasn't sure even spoke Spanish.

Bridge had a strict policy against bullying: To stand by and do nothing while a kid was getting bullied was almost as bad as doing the bullying yourself, and for a teacher – it was worse. Somewhere amid a flurry of meetings and phone calls and more meetings and phone calls, all of which Max's parents regularly updated him about, it was determined that Mr. Raymundo should have known better and was guilty of condoning the bullying of Max Buras.

Even with all this, though, somehow Max was feeling more confident than ever. His parents had promised to buy him LASIK surgery for his 14th birthday, and he was still going to the Y to look for his pecs every other day, with and without Rock Bromley. He had noticed his pants falling looser around the thighs and waist, his shirts fitting tighter around the chest and shoulders.

He was leaving his geeky old self behind.

✿ ✿ ✿

On the last day of winter break, they went sledding. Boise usually was not very snowy, what with "global warming" or "climate change," and Max knew they might not get a better chance.

"Max! I think you're growing!"

His mother held his old snowsuit in front of him. Max hadn't realized that in addition to slowly and painstakingly finding his pecs he might also be growing vertically. But he was.

"I think you've shot up a couple of inches!"

A trip to Play It Again Sports yielded a new snowsuit and a new, very white ski hat that his mom liked but that Max worried made him look like a girl.

His mother stayed home to clean the house while Max, Gabe, Sadie and Andy piled into the back of Dewey's cruiser. They drove to the infamous Simplot Hill, which was both the perfect sledding hill and the last place in the world kids should ever go sledding.

It was perfect because it was as steep as an intermediate-advanced ski run at nearby Bogus Basin, but less than perfect because it often spit sleds into traffic on Bogus Basin Road.

Andy wore a hat with moose antlers and woofed on the ride over that his sled was going to be the fastest sled, thanks to something to do with thermal dynamics, snowmelt, "glide radio," and the difference between anodized stainless steel and molded plastic.

Fastest was not important, Max wanted to say; at Simplot Hill, *safe* was what was important.

But he didn't say it. He didn't want to sound like a wussy.

"You're going down, Hastings," Max told Andy, trying to get into the spirit of it.

The sun shone on the packed powder, and Max hiked about a third of the way up and wondered if he shouldn't be wearing sunglasses. No one started from the top; there would be absolutely no way to keep from spilling out onto the road at the bottom, and then you just had to get lucky and hope you hit a lull in the traffic and not a car, parked or otherwise.

There were a dozen or more other kids out there with sleds; you could see their sled tracks from the thinner patches of snowmelt and the odd blade of grass poking up toward the sun.

Max looked at his breath in the air. He recognized a few voices, and then faces through drawn hoods—other kids from school. Everyone was so bundled up in parkas and snowsuits and gloves and Gore-Tex it was a little hard to tell who was who, but he could hear the difference between Gabe and Sadie and Andy, and Dewey was the tall one.

Sadie had taken the first run and had just begun to make her way back up, trudging toward them, when Dewey gave Gabe a push and sent him screaming down the hill both literally and otherwise. "Maybe not so hard," Max almost said just prior to the push.

But he didn't, and watched from on high as Gabe tore down the hill, headed for the road, but smartly bailed out at the last minute. He tumbled and slid along the surface of the snow as his red, rocket sled careened sideways and launched over a berm, into the air and disappeared from view.

It was the red sled against the white snow, Max later realized, that temporarily diverted his attention from his brother, who to Max's horror continued skimming along the packed snow, a blur of cartwheeling purple that launched off a mogul at the bottom, sailed into the abyss and—out of view, but not out of earshot—slammed into something big with a percussive and sickening *thwack*.

Max screamed, but couldn't hear any sound. Dewey, running down the hill, was already halfway to the road. All three of them were there in an instant, with Andy still making his way down behind them.

"Gabe! Gabe! Gabe! Wake up!"

Andy pulled up beside them and put his hands on his knees, looking down at the crumpled Gabe. The four of them stood huddled and horrified.

"Wake up!" Dewey said again as if that was the problem, Gabe had just fallen asleep in a weird place.

"Whoa," Andy said.

"Oh, my God," Sadie said. "Oh, my God. Oh, my God."

Max heard his heartbeat in his frozen ears and knelt down next to his brother to at least put a mitten under his head.

Gabe was sprawled on his back, in his purple snowsuit, the hood still drawn tight around his ears. They were in the bike lane on Bogus Basin Road, in the shadow of a parked, white camper van that apparently had no one in it.

Max gulped at the air. Sadie was crying next to him. Andy just stood there, and Dewey kept looking back and forth from Gabe to the parked Crown

Vic, which had to be about a quarter mile away—about a 100 yards down Bogus Basin toward town, and then, after a right turn, around 300 yards up Cartwright Road toward Hidden Springs.

A trickle of blood ran down Gabe's nose, which Max tried to stanch with his white hat. His brother had sustained a nasty bruise above his eye, too, but at least it wasn't bleeding. His eyes were still closed.

"I'm gonna make a run for it," Dewey said. "Get the car."

"Hurry up!" Sadie said. "He's turning cold!"

She had her hand on Gabe's forehead, and Max found himself studying her pink, raw, chapped looking fingers. He took his hat off of Gabe's nose, which seemed to have stopped bleeding, and folded it into a square pillow for his brother's head, tucking it between his purple hood and the sand and pebble-strewn frozen asphalt. One of Gabe's mittens had come off.

"Wait!" Max said.

Dewey turned around. He'd gotten only five or 10 feet toward the car.

"I'll be right back. I've got to get the car. We've got to get him to the ER."

"Don't go," Max said.

"Max," Dewey said, "no one's coming for us! My cell is in the car! We can't just stay out here!"

A small scrum of sledders had gathered, gawking at the dead boy and murmuring and shaking their heads. An older girl had retrieved Gabe's red sled and held it under her arm.

"Is there a doctor?" Sadie looked up at them, still with her hand on Gabe's forehead.

"A doctor! A doctor! A doctor?"

No one spoke. And that was when Dewey threw himself in front of traffic.

It happened so fast Max didn't have any time to stop him, not that he could have. Dewey went right out into the middle of Bogus Basin Road, and there was a screeching of tires, and the next thing Max knew Dewey was talking the driver of a red Mazda SUV and pointing at Gabe.

Dewey ran back to them.

"Okay, Jeff here is going to bring us to the hospital." Dewey nodded in the direction of the red Mazda, but it was gone. The guy, Jeff, had driven off.

"Take your glove off," Max said.

"What? No. We need to find someone to take us all to the hospital."

Dewey looked into Max's eyes, as if searching for a glimmer of understanding. "C'mon, Max, we've got to go to the—"

"Take your glove off," Max said again.

Dewey did.

"Over here, I mean," Max said.

Dewey knelt down next to Max and Gabe and Sadie. Andy was still frozen in place in his ridiculous moose hat.

"Okay, now, um, this is going to sound weird," Max continued, wondering if this was really going to work, "but put his hand in yours so it's up off the snow and the road and not freezing cold."

Dewey did as he was told.

"Now give Sadie the keys, she'll go get the car and bring it around."

Dewey looked at Max like he had three heads, and Sadie turned to her brother and sat up straight. "I'll what?"

Max was looking at his sister and formulating his response when heard Dewey, "Hey, there Gabe."

"Whoa," Andy said.

Max looked down at his brother, whose hand was mostly lost amid Dewey's long fingers. Gabe's eyes seemed to focus. He smiled.

"Gabe!" Max said.

"Max," Gabe said.

"Gabe, we thought we lost you," Dewey said.

"Oh, Gabe, baby," Sadie said.

"Gabe!" Max said.

"Max!"

"That was an EPIC run, buddy!" Max said.

Gabe rolled off Max's new white hat, which was now a blood-stained mess, and Sadie put her hand back on his forehead and rearranged the wet bangs spilling over his forehead. "Oh, Gabe. Are you okay?"

Gabe looked up at Dewey, and then at the gathering crowd of strangers. "Epic run," Gabe said, and Max exhaled and even laughed, which triggered a wave a relieved laughter all around.

"Epic run," Max repeated. He lifted his glasses up off his head and tried to steady his breathing.

"Boise Fry Company," Dewey said. "Let's go. This calls for hot cocoa. I'm buying."

"Yay!" Sadie said, trying to rally Gabe, who smiled.

"The price is right," Andy said.

"But we're going to the doctor's as soon as we're done," Dewey said.

"Hot cocoa!" Gabe said. "And fries!"

CHAPTER 22

He's not going to apologize.

Max sat in Mrs. McQuaid's office and looked out the window at Alan Whiting's parked Lexus SUV, that ridiculous car. The white paint job was almost invisible under the red, white and blue scrim job announcing the 2022 U.S. Open at The Country Club in Brookline, some golf course in Massachusetts.

Of all the ways Max had imagined spending the first Friday after the Christmas break, chief among them was probably sitting on a beach with Susannah Jurevicious, sipping drinks with pineapple amid the echo of ukulele music wafting in on the warm breeze. Sitting in the cramped office of the Bridge Academy principal, next to his dad and opposite Alan Whiting and his golf prodigy son Pete, who had led the bloodless coup to strip Max of his managerial duties with the team, well, it would've rated 101st on a list of 100.

But there they were.

Max and Pete remained mostly silent as their fathers opened with firm handshakes and deep voices and some small talk about the real estate market and the weather and the bowl chances for the Boise State football team.

"Why don't you four make yourselves at home," Mrs. McQuaid said, looking at a blinking light on her phone. "I've got to take this. I'll be back in just a sec."

She slipped out her office door and closed it, leaving the four of them to sit there in silent regard for the awful facts and what to do about them.

"I believe your son," Max's dad said before stopping himself. He turned to Pete. "I believe you owe Max an apology."

"Pete owes you nothing," Alan shot back.

Max squirmed in his seat—so much for pleasantries.

"Pete is going to do whatever he has to do to get that little white ball into the hole as fast as possible, and I trust him to know what that is."

"Oh, and that means throwing my son under the bus?" Max looked at his mild-mannered father anew. His cheeks were full of color, there was rage in his eyes, and Max was fairly certain he'd never seen his dad like this.

"We drive a van, not a bus," Max joked. Nobody laughed or even cracked a smile, but at least he'd said something on his behalf, sort of.

"Pete did not throw anyone under the bus," Alan said. "He merely did what he thought was best for the team. This is not about Pete, and it's not about Max here. Am I right? It's about the team. There's no 'I' in team."

No 'I' in team. What a dumb cliché. Max fought back a smile as he looked over at Pete Whiting, who was slumped in his chair and studying the carpet, a glazed look on his face, as if he'd just shot another ghastly 88.

"Pete," Max's father said. "Your father and I have gone around and around on this matter, both over the phone and now here, and although we've made a valiant effort, we don't seem to be getting any closer to a resolution. I'd like to hear your side of this, if you don't mind."

Mrs. McQuaid opened the door, entered, and closed it behind her. "I do apologize," she said.

"Okay," she continued, stepping behind her giant desk and pulling back her chair. "Someone is going to need to catch me up."

"I was just saying there's no 'I' in team," Alan Whiting said.

"Why doesn't Max catch me up?"

Max looked over at Pete Whiting, who was now glaring at his own father.

"Well," Max said. "That's true. Mr. Whiting said there's no 'I' in team, and there seems to be a consensus that the BSU football team might get in the Chick-fil-A Bowl, and the real estate market is quote-unquote humming along, and I said we don't drive a bus, we drive a van, the golf team, I mean, and—well, that's, um, I don't know. I think that's everything."

Max scanned the room for confirmation, but no one spoke. He eyed his favorite new Christmas clothes, courtesy of personal shopper Judy Buras—multi-colored, striped sweater over red collared shirt (with cool pattern), plus warm, gray wool pants. If Alan or Pete Whiting were to pull out a 9-iron or something and club him to death, which seemed entirely possible, at least he'd look good.

"I can see you're all going to need a nudge in the right direction," Mrs. McQuaid said. "Peter Whiting, I believe you owe Max an apology."

"What?" Alan looked like Godzilla had just stepped on his Lexus.

"That's what I've been saying all along," Max's father said. He could have said so much more, it must have been tempting to gloat, but he didn't, and Max admired his dad's restraint.

Max looked at Alan, who had crossed his arms and was silent for the first time. Max's father was looking squarely at Pete, who still hadn't said a word since they'd got here, and soon Max was looking at him, too, and so was Mrs. McQuaid and so was Mr. Whiting.

"I'm sorry!" Pete said.

But Max didn't believe it. He didn't know which was worse, that he'd had to pretend this all might end amicably, or that he was now supposed to pretend to believe Pete Whiting was well and truly sorry.

"I'm going to ask you to say that again," Mrs. McQuaid said. "And this time I'll ask you to look Max in the eye and say it as if you really are sorry, not just sorry to have to say you're sorry."

"Oh, come on," Alan said. "He said he's sorry."

"Alan," Mrs. McQuaid said, and he looked at his knees. To Max's way of thinking, at least, it was starting to seem as if Mr. Whiting had spent some time in the principal's office, too, in his day.

"I'm sorry," Pete said again, this time without quite so much anger.

"Max?" Mrs. McQuaid looked at him from across her desk.

Max turned to face Pete. "Apology accepted."

Mrs. McQuaid stood up and beamed. "There! Doesn't everyone feel better? Max, you're of course free to change your mind and rejoin the team in the position of manager if it fits with your spring schedule, but I believe this closes the book on the unfortunate events at the district tournament."

The rest of them followed her lead and stood up, gathering coats and hats and gloves.

"Not quite," Alan Whiting said.

CHAPTER TWENTY THREE

The smile disappeared from Mrs. McQuaid's face. "Oh?"

"There's still no coach," Alan said.

"And so there isn't," Mrs. McQuaid said. "And since it's still January, and there's still snow on the ground, we're going to table that decision until the spring. At Bridge we cross our bridges when we come to them."

She offered a polite smile, and Alan Whiting and Max's father shook hands, Max shook hands with Pete and Alan, Pete shook hands with Max's father, everyone shook hands with Mrs. McQuaid.

It was all very complicated.

Max wondered if Mrs. McQuaid had any early candidates to replace Mr. Raymundo, and if she had any working knowledge of golf at all, and, if she didn't, who at the school did.

He never in a million years could have predicted how that one would work itself out.

CHAPTER

The start of winter term was marked by the arrival of a new transfer student from New York named Ed Hocking, who now sat one row to Max's right in math. Hocking was also myopic, like Max, and with almost the same prescription in his glasses. He had blond hair, thick eyebrows, and was tall. He said he planned to go out for golf in the spring.

Max filled him in on how he had been the team manager until he'd been voted out, and how it had been a 3-2 decision, and how Hadley Jackson had come to his defense but Max had never found out who had cast the other vote in his favor. He told Hocking how Pete Whiting had delivered the bad news, and how Pete was Bridge Academy's No. 1 golfer, and Ed Hocking listened to all of this. He seemed more sophisticated than the other kids, or maybe they just talked differently in New York, because a few days later, after having observed Pete in the hallways and around campus, Ed Hocking said, "That guy is definitely more bacon than the pan can handle."

Was it an insult? A compliment? Max had no idea, but nodded as if he understood perfectly.

When he wasn't doing homework or throwing medicine balls around with Rock Bromley at the Y, Max burrowed into the living room couch at home for extended sessions with "SyberVision Men's Muscle Memory Programming for Golf with Al Geiberger."

No way would Max ever swing a golf club like Al Geiberger, but he found the DVD strangely relaxing, as did Gabe, who seemed to be able to watch the little white ball fly off Al's club, in slow motion and from multiple angles and all to a mesmerizing sound track, for hours on end.

At the Y, Max was becoming increasingly confident in his abilities at Rock Bromley's Hammer Throw Boot Camp, maybe because he'd been working out on his own. Although nowhere near the marks of two-time state champion Ivor Jenks, his medicine ball throws were flying farther, as was the pretend "hammer," which was made out of a rope attached to a vinyl-covered beanbag so as not to splinter the Boise High gymnasium floor.

"I like it!" Rock Bromley sometimes said. And sometimes he said, "Yeah, man! Way to go, M!"

No one had ever called Max "M" before. He liked the name even if he wasn't sure he was doing anything that warranted special recognition. The Y was an easy 10 minute walk from his house, except when it snowed. The staff had started to recognize him and always seemed happy to see him.

He may not have shared a birthday with Dewey, but there was some *alchemy* going on within Max. It was called puberty. He was not only growing taller but he had started to see more and more evidence that he did indeed have pecs. Dewey was even helping him learn some of the machines at the YMCA, explaining what muscle groups they targeted.

If the scale in the Y locker room was correct, Max had put on just over eight pounds, which Rock Bromley said was probably due to a gain of about 12 pounds of muscle and a loss of four pounds of fat. Max's arms and his shoulders and his "traps" ached—"traps" was a muscle in his back, according to Rock Bromley—but Max liked the feeling, the perpetual soreness confirming he was growing out of his old self.

One day in late February he ran into Alex Fisk, Hadley Jackson, Don Kennerly, Phil Hendrickson and Peter Whiting. Max had always heard of the virtues of "off-season training" for golfers, but as team manager he'd never actually ventured down to the Y with the guys.

"Max!" Hadley said, offering a knuckle-bump.

Max connected with Hadley's fist. "Hi, guys."

Pete Whiting adjusted something on one of his taped wrists, and examined his chalked hands. He wore a navy-blue, short-sleeved Nike T-shirt with white block letters—"Train insane or remain the same"—and navy-blue Nike shorts with white compression shorts underneath, and new looking Nike sneakers, also navy-blue and white.

Max felt hopelessly unfashionable in his billowy, red sweatpants, which had a hole in the right knee, and a blue and orange BSU sweatshirt they'd found on the clearance rack at Ross Dress For Less.

"You lifting, Buras?"

Max felt the first wave of fear. Was he lifting? Well, yes, sort of, nothing special, not breaking any records or anything.

"Um," he said.

"Max Buras is lifting," Pete said.

"Yes?" Max felt pleased to have finally formed a word.

Pete looked him up and down, took a quick glance at his teammates, and then addressed Max again.

"Cool," he said.

CHAPTER 24

Wood grain. Max had never noticed wood grain before, but as he stood on Andy's doorstep, Max let his eyes follow the black-stained wood grain around the perimeter of his modernist-style front door with its frosted-glass panels—three of them, stacked horizontally on top of each other—and sleek, L-shaped chrome handle.

The door swung open. "Whoa," Andy said.

"Yeah," Max said. He smiled, shrugged. "Welcome to the new me, right?"

"How does it feel?"

"Good. I mean, normal, sort of. It's like they're still up there."

It had been about 48 hours since he'd had LASIK surgery, the long-awaited life-changer that his parents had promised him when he turned 14, and now he was wondering if this was what it felt like to have a phantom limb. He saw as sharply and as clearly as if he were wearing his glasses, but they were, like, invisible glasses. He kept reaching for them, but they weren't there, and his hand found only his freshly shorn hair—No. 2 clippers on the side and back, a little longer on the top.

"But they're not up there," Max continued.

"They're not!" Andy said. "I almost didn't recognize you!"

His Seattle Seahawks jersey was way too big for him, his protruding breastbone visible above the sagging V-neck. The jersey hung low over the waist of his thinly corrugated beige corduroys.

"Come on in. I'm just about ready."

Andy's house was roasting hot, as usual, and smelled like dinner.

"Hi, Max!" Mr. Hastings, who looked like he'd been trying to grow a beard, was sunken into the forest-green couch in the living room and peeked out from behind his *Fortune* magazine. "Big game tonight?"

"Hi, Mr. H. Yeah, I guess. Bridge volleyball is kind of a big deal these days. District finals and all that—I hope we win."

Mr. Hastings pointed to his face. "Got rid of your glasses, eh?"

"Yeah."

"Good for you. You just missed chicken tortilla soup. Would you like some? Barbara! We have enough to feed the entire 10th Mountain Division."

"Oh, no, that's fine. I'm fine. I just ate."

Mr. H turned to face the stairs again. "Never mind!"

"It smells good, though," Max said.

"Barbara's going to a movie with a girlfriend. Or her other husband!" He laughed, flicked something off his pant leg. "Andy tells me you've been working out?"

Max scrunched up his nose. "Yeah."

For some reason he felt sort of apologetic about it, about not being the same kid who'd been Andy's best friend, who'd whiled away all those after-school hours playing Ping-Pong and Scrabble.

"Good for you," Mr. H said again. He went back to his magazine.

Mr. H was in finance. He wore finely creased slacks and a monogrammed, pink shirt with cuff links.

Max appraised his own outfit: jeans and his favorite shirt, the red one with the cool pattern. It still fit him but not by much, especially in the neck and shoulders. Sadie said that meant it actually fit him better.

Gabe, in the midst of a video game kick and out at a video game arcade called Dave & Busters tonight with Dewey, didn't much care one way or the other what he wore, much less Max's fashion choices.

Dewey wore mountaineering boots and was disqualified from having a say.

In a way, picking out what to wear to watch a school sporting event was more important than picking out what to wear to prom, where a standard tuxedo left little room for improvisation.

Max, recalling the "wisdom of the hive mind," a phrase he'd heard on the Discovery Channel, had solicited input from every family member. The risk was that his parents would misinterpret this as an invitation to join him, but they'd been acting pretty distracted lately, again with the hushed tones, and Max had failed in his furtive attempts to hear their conversations through the bathroom wall.

His new jeans were a no-brainer. Of course he'd worn those. They had cool stitching around the back pockets, and a button fly, and they too, had been a gift for his birthday, what with his having grown a few inches. He'd talked his mother into the slightly more expensive brand.

They'll last longer, he said.

They're cooler, he didn't say.

But they were.

❋ ❋ ❋

The last of the winter snow had melted and temperatures were rising so Max and Andy biked to the game. Max's parents had made him wear so many lights he looked like a lit-up Christmas tree—"You'd better hope no pilots mistake you for an airport runway," Andy joked—and after the LASIK surgery, Max felt almost as if he was seeing through infrared goggles.

"It feels weird," he said as they biked through a green light at State Street. "But weird in a good way."

Andy snuck a quick look at him. "You had those things on your face so long I honestly couldn't have told you what color your eyes were. I mean, like, you had *polycarbonate* eyes."

"I guess I don't look like Kurt Rambis anymore," Max said.

"Who?"

"The Los Angeles Lakers guy you showed me a picture of."

Andy's face showed no glimmer of understanding. Max laughed. "Never mind."

Navy and white banners hung from the ceiling of the Bridge gymnasium, and the band was already belting out the Hawaii Five-O theme song, and the cheerleaders were cheerleading, and Max's pulse quickened as he watched Susannah Jurevicious take her final warm-up spikes at net.

"Hey, watch it!"

Oops. Max looked down and realized that in venturing into the shiny wooden bleachers, which were mostly already full, he had stepped on Lilly Robinson's foot. She was sitting next to her brother, Freddy, on one side, and Graham Godwin on the other.

"Sorry," Max said, wondering what Sadie would make of Graham Godwin going to the game with Lilly. "Excuse us—just getting to our seats, coming through, coming through, coming through."

"Buras," Freddy said. "What happened to the specs?"

Max smiled. "I've been eating a lot of carrots," he said before continuing through the packed risers.

Susannah was huddled up with the rest of the team now, the starters standing and out of their navy-blue warm-ups: white jerseys with numbered backs, skimpy white shorts, long legs. The entire team huddled up, arms over their heads as if tethered to a tent pole. "Bridge!"

The Star Christian girls, in red and white, waited patiently on the other side of the net.

"Hey, Buras! What happened to the Coke bottles?"

Anton Willoughby, the center of the Bridge basketball team, was on his feet about 10 rows up, amid a large group of fellow basketball players in addition to some football players and a few guys from the golf team.

"I recycled them!" Max yelled. Anton, who spearheaded the school's recycling efforts, gave a thumbs-up.

Max, who had never known Anton even knew his name, found a clear spot in the bleachers that was a little bit off to the side and a little bit high. Good enough. A week ago the game would have been a fuzzy approximation of limbs and net and ball, with Max relying on the sound of the crowd to tell him what had happened. But now he could see fine.

Andy joined him a few minutes later, loaded down with refreshments.

"Geez," Andy said, throwing a small packet into Max's lap before handing him a sweating bottle of water. "I can't believe all you wanted was water and corn nuts."

Andy held up a jumbo sack of popcorn and a large soda. "Don't tell Rock Bromley about this."

As soon as the match began Susannah Jurevicious wasted no time asserting her dominance. She leaped high over the net and spiked the ball between two startled looking Star Christian defenders, the ball smacking the hardwood floor with a loud report before bounding into the bleachers.

The home crowd roared.

"Yes!" Max said. He looked down to find he was standing.

"Geez," Andy said. "Calm down. It's only the first point."

But that was how most of the points went, or so it seemed. Susannah Jurevicious finished the game with a game-high 17 kills. (Max counted, in case maybe she needed someone up here in the stands keeping stats for her.) Bridge won the match, and the district title, 15-7, 16-14, 15-7.

The horn section of the band played Queen's "We Are the Champions" as the players shook hands and the crowd filed out and some guy on the P.A. system said to "drive safe" and Max and Andy slowly made their way to the exit, with Max craning his neck to maintain a visual on Susannah Jurevicious.

"Dude," Andy said. "Where are you going?"

"I'm just—I'm just, wait up for me."

Max's heart beat wildly as his legs carried him onto the court, where he realized his mouth was woefully short of saliva. He didn't belong here. Oh, to be one of the popular kids.

"Hi," he said. Jeez. *Hi.* He was so lame. Was that all he could think to say?

She looked down at him. There was an awful, sticky paste in his mouth, and Max cursed the corn nuts.

"Um," he tried again. "Good game?"

Susannah Jurevicious was glistening, the blood up in her cheeks, her hair damp. She wiped her brow with her long shirtsleeve. Someone said something from across the gym and she waved. "Thanks!" she said, waving back.

She looked at Max.

"Sorry. Who are you?"

Max felt his face get red, heard a ringing in his ears, watched his newly perfect vision blur into a kaleidoscope of fuzzy fractals. And here he'd been feeling hopeful what with Bridge winning and Max now almost as tall as Susannah Jurevicious's nose.

"It's me. Max. Max Buras." Gawd. He hoped he wouldn't pass out.

Andy pulled up next to them. "Hey," he said, out of breath.

Oh, great.

Susannah smiled, her eyes finally registering. "Max Buras? From Spanish class—that Max?" Again, a wave of dizziness came over him. Flaxen-haired, long-legged goddess of the volleyball court Susannah Jurevicious was smiling at him.

"Yeah! It's me!" he said. Geez, he really had a way with words tonight.

"Sorry," she said. "I already took my contacts out."

"Oh, that's okay. This is Andy. I think you guys had Comparative Religions together last year?"

"Hey," Andy said.

"You look different," Susannah said.

"Yeah," Max said. "I guess I had LASIK and all that."

Geez. He *guessed* he had LASIK? He was there! He HAD the LASIK!

"I ditched the glasses," he said.

"Yeah, you did! I almost didn't recognize you!"

"You didn't recognize me," Max said. He laughed.

"Yeah, like I said, I didn't recognize you!" Now she laughed. "You look good, Max."

Max tried to make a word, but he'd forgotten how to talk.

"Call me sometime," Susannah Jurevicious said over her shoulder as she rejoined her teammates.

Wait. What? Who? Call? When?

"Whoa," Andy said.

Max tried to force some air across his dry tongue and into his lungs as Susannah Jurevicious mingled with family members and friends, all of whom were infinitely more popular than Max and Andy.

"Whoa," Andy said again. "Hey, what the—"

Without looking away from the vision of perfection that was Susannah Jurevicious, Max grabbed Andy's soda, which was now mostly water, and took a few desperate and noisy pulls on the straw. "Sorry, but that was a life or death situation. Corn nuts. Salty."

Max would remember exactly nothing about their bike ride home. All he wanted to do was be still and let his mind attempt to process the events of the evening, maybe plop down and veg in front of the TV, maybe watch some "SyberVision Men's Muscle Memory Programming for Golf with Al Geiberger," maybe with Gabe. So it seemed particularly unfair, given his state of disequilibrium, to walk right into the middle of a family meeting.

❀ ❀ ❀

"We'd like to try Gabe at Bridge."

Max and Sadie, seated at opposite ends of the living room couch, looked across at their parents, in a pair of brown, reupholstered chairs.

"Unless you two have any objections," their mom continued, "in which case we can talk about that. But your dad and I have gone over this and we believe that Gabe is doing much, much better, and this is the natural next step. We've contacted Mrs. McQuaid, and they have the resources."

Max felt a wave of panic and hated himself for it. Still, the thought persisted: *Just when I was starting to get popular at Bridge.*

It seemed weird and sort of wrong to have a family meeting without Gabe, but he was still out at Dave & Busters, playing video games, with Dewey.

"I don't know," Sadie said. "I mean, geez, are you sure? What if he's not ready? I don't mean he's not smart, but Bridge is kind of, like, all academically challenging and everything. And he's doing so well as is. Why rock the boat?"

Max looked across the couch at his sister, who seemed to be having the same feelings as him.

Sadie continued: "I mean, what if it's a disaster?"

"If it's a disaster," their dad said, "then we pull him out and send him back to Circle of Friends. Nothing is ever set in stone. But we don't think it'll be a disaster."

"Why?" Max said.

"Because we think he's ready," their dad said. "And we want him to be around kids with more neuro-typical behaviors so he can see what those look like, and we have reason to believe this school will be better for him in one big way immediately."

He smiled at their mom.

"That's right," she said. "We see this as sort of a two-for-one deal."

Max left it to his sister, the oldest one, after all, to ask the obvious if slightly impertinent question. "What on earth are you guys talking about?" she said.

Good old Sadie—he could always count on her to cut the baloney.

"We think the timing is right," their mother said, "in part because a janitorial position just came open at the school. It's only part-time; Dewey will still be working at the YMCA in the mornings, but he'll be at Bridge for the majority of the school day."

Dewey. Gabe. Bio-harmonic convergence. Max felt a smile creep up on him. "Okay," he said. "This oughta be interesting."

CHAPTER 25

Somewhere along the line, in early March, Dewey had taken Gabe to Jackpot, Nevada, and won $5,710 playing craps. The way Dewey told the story, they were in and out of that place before anyone realized that at 10 years old Gabe wasn't even old enough to be allowed in the room.

Dewey told Max in late March as the three of them made their way to Warm Springs Golf Course in the police cruiser. Max did the math. Since Jackpot was a day trip from Boise, a couple hours there and a couple hours back, Dewey had to have pulled Gabe out of school and gotten someone in the office to write it up as a sick day. It had to have been fairly easy, since Dewey always drove Gabe to and from school each day, anyway.

"Listen, it'll be our secret, just the boys," Dewey said with a wink on the drive to Warm Springs. "Okay?"

Max and Gabe nodded.

"Just between you and me and that road sign over there, janitorial work doesn't pay all that well," Dewey continued. "It requires a little *supplementation.*"

To Max the whole thing sounded naughty, but Dewey used the Jackpot winnings to pay for all new clubs for Max and Gabe, top of the line, plus new golf bags with kickstands and multiple pockets. Max had always used his dad's clubs. Gabe had never had clubs. Dewey said he had bought *his* clubs at a yard sale in Oregon and still hadn't upgraded.

Dewey pulled the old police cruiser into the parking lot. It was one of those spring Saturdays where everyone in the world seems to wake up to the urgent need to get outside, and the driving range was a whirl of activity, the sound and smell of gas-powered golf carts and the smell of fresh-cut grass and hot dogs wafting in over the crowd of hopeful hackers.

Max felt the beginnings of sweat on his arms and torso, under his new golf shirt. Ed Hocking, the transfer student from New York, was hitting balls at the end of the range, and Max could see from Hocking's syrupy, textbook swing that Pete Whiting was going to have to fight to keep his No. 1 spot. Dewey bought three tokens from a bearded guy in the pro shop, and from a box-shaped metal vending machine just outside the door and down the steps he filled up three large buckets of beat up range balls. Max found them three open stalls.

"It's a simple game," Dewey said as his gums worked a piece of bubble gum, his new vice as he tried to quite smoking. He blew a bubble, reared back and blistered a ball low and true, and Max watched as it buzzed the big "200" sign and skidded to a stop amid the others in the grass.

"Nice one," Max said.

Dewey's swing was far from textbook. In fact, it had so many moving parts it reminded Max of one of those arm-flailing, inflatable wiggle men that towered over car dealerships. But it worked.

Max tugged at the bill of his cap and pulled a 5-iron out of his bag. He took a practice swing, savoring the whooshing noise the club made as it cut through the air. His exposed forearms and legs looked different now—still winter-white, but more defined than they'd ever been thanks to his sessions at the Y. He put a ball down. First shot of the year. He took a deep breath, steadied his head, reared back and hoped for the best.

Crack! The mishit sent a shock up his forearms, and Max watched as his ball sliced right and into an enormous web of netting.

"Ouch," Dewey said. He blew a bubble.

"Yeah," Max said, shaking his hands.

Gabe had had to go the bathroom as soon as they got here, but now he sauntered up and set his Transformers golf bag in the stall behind Max.

"Sunscreen." Max placed a blob of white goop on Gabe's nose, and the boy winced and tried to turn away as his older brother rubbed it all the way in.

"The big man!" Dewey said, looking at Gabe and then at his watch. "Now on the tee with the 11:15 a.m. starting time, from U.S.A., Gabe Buras!"

Gabe smiled and worked a new, white glove onto his hand. In addition to the junior set of clubs, Dewey had bought Gabe a white newsboy cap, the kind

Ben Hogan used to wear. Gabe drew a club out of his bag and moved into his stall. He gave a few waggles.

"Nice waggle," Dewey said.

The swing that followed was unlike anything Max had ever seen—with the notable exception of "SyberVision Men's Muscle Memory Programming for Golf with Al Geiberger." The ball made a crisp, flush sound as it came off Gabe's 5-iron.

The ball soared into the air, reached its pinnacle against the cloudless, blue sky, and came to rest just behind the "150" sign. With his club, Gabe rolled another ball onto the fake green grass, took his stance, reared back, and hit the same shot—same sound, trajectory and destination.

Dewey turned to Max. "You said he'd never played before?"

"Uh, no, unless my dad's been taking him. But I'd have heard about it."

Gabe hit his third straight perfect 5-iron into the warm air and they watched the ball fall behind the "150" sign.

"Huh," Dewey said.

"Yeah, huh," Max said.

"I guess he had no bad habits."

"Guess not."

"Looks like you've got a prodigy there!"

Max turned around to find a middle-aged woman with tight polyester pants, a long-sleeved, button-down beige top, and an ample mop of snowy hair spilling out from under a green visor.

"Oh, hi, Mrs. McQuaid—Principal McQuaid, I mean."

"Just Mrs. McQuaid is fine," she said, her eyes on Gabe.

Li'l Geiberger hit another perfect 5-iron.

"Quite a swing," she said.

"It's his first time," Max said.

Mrs. McQuaid laughed. "Yeah, right. And I sang backup for Aretha Franklin."

She eyed Dewey. "You just started working at the school, no? The janitorial position?"

"I did! Yes, yes, that's where I recognize you from—context!"

They shook hands.

"Ah, yes," Mrs. McQuaid said, addressing Dewey. "You know the Buras family. You take care of Gabe here, our newest fifth grader at Bridge."

Gabe was still rifling 5-irons out into the horizon like a machine.

"Guilty as charged," Dewey said. He blew a bubble, which popped and stuck to his lips. "Excuse me," he said, tidying it up with his tongue.

Mrs. McQuaid laughed and eyed Dewey for an extra beat.

"Your resume said you used to drive a tow truck?"

Dewey brightened. "Good memory! Yes, I did."

"You need a commercial license for that?"

"Oh, yeah," Dewey said. "I'm all up to date there."

"Huh," Mrs. McQuaid said. She turned to Gabe, who was now hitting a fairway metal at the 175 sign.

"I didn't know you played golf," Max said.

Mrs. McQuaid turned to him and smiled. "Oh, you know. Far away, there in the sunshine, are my highest aspirations. I may not reach them, but…"

She looked at Max.

"Louisa May Alcott," she said.

"Right!" Max said.

Dewey looked up. "Didn't she play on LPGA Tour?"

"That was Amy Alcott," Mrs. McQuaid said.

She walked back toward her hitting bay and a full bucket of balls. "I'll see you all at school!"

Max didn't know she meant in her office. Again.

CHAPTER 26

Dewey had begun dating Cynthia, Gabe's speech pathologist. To judge his buoyant mood, this made him happy. It certainly would have made Max happy. Cynthia wasn't beautiful, or at least not Max's idea of beautiful, but she was really nice.

Also, Dewey had settled into his new part-time job at Bridge, the kids liked him, and Gabe liked his new teacher, a 25-year-old woman with a kind, round face and the patience of a saint.

Gabe was "settling in," as Max's mom put it. They all were. Dewey was getting more serious about his stated desire to climb the Grand Tetons in Wyoming, spending time testing equipment, scouring maps and attending talks at the REI out by the mall. Also, he finally got new teeth. They were dazzlingly white, like something you might see sitting in a glass of bubbling water in a dentures commercial, but he seemed pleased with them.

"All I gotta do is get to work on drinking that coffee," he told Max. "Put some stains on these babies so they don't damage people's retinas."

He'd managed to stay off the cigarettes, thanks to copious amounts of bubble gum, and he said he'd started a tenants-rights group at the Grandview Motel.

Max had not called Susannah Jurevicious, and he told himself this was because he didn't know her number. He also wasn't sure if she had really wanted him to call or not. *Call me sometime.* It sounded like one of those overused, meaningless phrases like *I love your work.* Or was it?

Rock Bromley was trying to convince the newly buff Max to go out for track and specifically the hammer throw, but Max knew how much time and effort it would require, and it would be a steep climb to even make the varsity let alone challenge No. 1 thrower Ivor Jenks.

Not that playing golf for Bridge was an option. Max was no better than he'd been before watching the instructional videos, but wrote a letter to Al Geiberger to say there was a kid in Boise—a quiet little boy named Gabe Buras who wore a white newsboy cap—who had gotten the great man's swing imprinted on his brain chip and now never missed a shot.

Sadie continued to seem happy pursuing "the theater arts," which in the spring meant a production of *Groundhog Day*. Max had seen the movie; he remembered liking it.

❋ ❋ ❋

Three trips to the principal's office in one year—Max wondered if this was a school record.

"Mr. Buras," Mrs. McQuaid said, closing the door behind her. "The Carnac of the M&M's. And Dewey Tomlinson, golf teacher extraordinaire."

"I didn't have anything to do with that," Dewey said of Gabe's preternatural golf ability. "That was Al Geiberger."

"Who?"

"Instructional video," Max clarified.

"I'll bet you two are wondering why you're here," Mrs. McQuaid said.

"Uh, yeah," Dewey said.

Mrs. McQuaid was standing under one of the words on her wall. DREAM, this one said in giant, multi-colored letters that appeared to be made of wood.

"As you know," she said, sitting back down at her desk, "we no longer have a golf coach after the unfortunate events at the end of the fall season."

"Right," Max said. "Mr. Raymundo."

Mrs. McQuaid traced her finger around the perimeter of her desk blotter. She looked up at them and smiled. "Gentlemen, I'll cut right to it: We need a golf coach."

Max saw that Dewey had stiffened in his seat.

"What's the matter, Mr. Tomlinson? You look as if you've just seen a ghost!"

"I told you," he said. "I'm no coach."

"You would only be the nominal coach," she said. "In fact I'd venture to guess you might only have to do the driving of the team van. Nothing more." She looked over at Max. "So long as Max here agrees to be reinstalled as team manager."

Max fidgeted in his seat. His stomach felt funny.

"I've given this a lot of thought," Mrs. McQuaid said. "I've spoken to everyone who would be impacted—your teammates, their parents and, yes, your parents, Max. Only one player's parent—and you can probably guess which one—opposed the idea."

"But I'm just a kid," Max said. "How can *I* lead the team? I'm only 13. Those guys don't even like me. They voted me off the island, remember?"

"Oh, nonsense." Mrs. McQuaid got up out of her seat and began to walk around amid all those words on her walls: PERSEVERE. DREAM. *EMPOWER.* "First of all, if anyone asks, you're not really the coach. Mr. Tomlinson is the coach. You're the manager, like before. I've spoken to your teammates, Max. I know what you did."

"What did I do?" Max said.

"As team manager," Mrs. McQuaid said. "I know you set up practices, reserved and announced the tee times, maintained the equipment and helped keep the van in working order. I understand you even used some of your own money to buy new golf balls—Titleist ProV1s, if I have my information correct. Those aren't cheap, are they?"

Again, Max squirmed in his seat. "We were running low."

"Right," Mrs. McQuaid pressed on. "And haven't they apologized to you?"

"Individually," Max said, "but not as a team."

"Well, listen," Mrs. McQuaid said, pulling her desk chair out and sitting back down to face them. "My point, Max, is that that's what a *coach* does. You did *two* jobs in the fall, yours and Mr. Raymundo's, and all I'm asking you to do for the next six weeks is keep doing it. And you, Mr. Tomlinson—"

She turned to face Dewey. "The job comes with a small stipend."

Mrs. McQuaid steepled her hands in front of her, cracking her knuckles.

"I'm sure the two of you will form quite a team, will *lead* quite a team, if you so choose. I see no reason why you shouldn't start right away. Do we have a deal?"

Max looked at Dewey; Dewey looked at Max.

"Uh, um," they stammered, cracking them both up.

Mrs. McQuaid stood up, beaming. "Is that a yes?"

"Fine by me," Dewey said.

Max smiled. "Yes," he said. "But on one condition."

CHAPTER 27

"You should change your name."

Sadie had her head in the iPad at breakfast, and Max wondered what bright new idea she was on to now. Her last burst of inspired thought had involved building a robot to sit next to her so she could drive without adult supervision.

"I mean, like, legally or whatever, change your name," Sadie added, nudging the last of her Cheerios with her spoon. "People do it all the time."

Their parents were at work, and since it was an "in-service" day at school, Max and Sadie had a free day. So did Gabe, who was still asleep.

"To what?" Max asked. "I sort of like Max. I'm used to it. And besides, I don't think changing my name to *Miles* or *Anthony* or something is the kind of thing Mom and Dad would probably get too excited about—at least not in a good way."

"Oh, you'd still be Max," Sadie said, looking up from the iPad. "Only you'd spell it with two Xs. M-a-x-x—with two Xs."

Max grinned. "Why?"

"Because a million guys are called Max! It's common! And you're not common." Sadie closed the iPad cover and set it aside. "You *were* common at the beginning of the school year, but you sure aren't anymore. You should be voted, like, *Least likely to resemble any part of your geeky self at the beginning of the school year*."

"Gee, thanks," Max said.

"Your welcome. The point is when you add an 'X' to anything it automatically becomes 30 percent cooler. Maybe more."

She opened up the iPad cover again. "Look at this guy: Francis X. Clines, writes for the *New York Times*."

"You read the *New York Times*?"

"Dad does. He left the iPad on one of his articles. Think about it, Max. The guy could've called himself just Francis Clines, which sounds like he should be wearing a pocket protector and teaching algebra, or Francis X. Clines, which sounds like he should be leading a resistance movement, like standing in front of bulldozers in the rain forest or mobilizing Congress to do something about those skinny kids in Africa."

"How do you know it's a he?" Max asked.

"I just assumed," Sadie said, her face awash in the light of the iPad.

"Oh, never mind," she added. "It says here you have to be 18 to change your name. Well *that* seems unfair. Sorry if I got your hopes up."

"You didn't get my hopes up," Max said.

She closed the iPad cover again. "I can't believe you're the golf coach now."

"I'm not the golf coach. Dewey is the golf coach. I just make all the decisions and he gets the stipend. If anybody asks, I'm the manager, like before, and he's the coach."

"That doesn't seem fair."

"I don't know what's fair anymore," Max said. "I just know the team apologized, and I accepted their apology, and we're an early favorite to win state this year."

Sadie got up and rinsed her cereal bowl and left it in the sink and left it in the sink and headed toward the bathroom to get ready for the day. "So I hear," she said over her shoulder.

Max wondered where and when and with whom Sadie had had the occasion to talk high school golf. He had to admit she was right—not about the *Maxx* thing but about the fact that he didn't really resemble the Max from the start of the school year. His body was no longer shaped like a bag of marshmallows, thanks to Rock Bromley. He'd sprouted up a few inches, and his head, absent his Coke-bottle glasses and the lame wrap-around strap to keep them on straight, no longer resembled a peanut.

If he had to testify on the witness stand, like on *Law & Order*, he'd have said these were factors in his decision to show up at auditions for *Groundhog Day*.

He'd have said he was feeling more confident in himself, although still highly nervous about the idea of memorizing his monologue and commanding the stage and correctly pronouncing his lines.

He'd have said that he'd gotten a kick out of the Bill Murray movie, as had Gabe, who mostly liked the groundhog, and that he was going to have some time now that he'd officially turned down Rock Bromley's invitation to throw the hammer as a sort of redshirted future prospect at Boise High.

But if he'd been dosed with truth serum, Max would have had to say it was Susannah Jurevicious and the rumor Sadie had heard that Bridge's most famous volleyball player, fresh off another state title-winning season, was going to try for the lead female role (played by Andie MacDowell in the movie).

Although he'd never felt any yearning to take the stage, Max now longed to be Bill Murray, the male lead, grumpy weatherman Phil Connors. He wanted it more than he'd wanted anything.

"He has a totally excellent piano solo at the end," he told Sadie.

But she smiled in a way that said she wasn't fooled. She knew it was because after reliving the same day over and over again Phil Connors finally gets it right and gets the girl, who was quite possibly going to be played by Susannah Jurevicious. "Piano solo," Sadie said, shaking her hand. "That's why you keep looking at yourself in the mirror?"

For Max there was only one role; it was going to be Phil Connors or nothing. The news cameraman character, whatever his name was, wouldn't kiss Susannah Jurevicious, nor would Ned Ryerson, the insurance salesman, or the Punxsutawney mayor. No, it was Phil Connors or nothing—because the thought of kissing Susannah Jurevicious made Max's heart swell and his head feel like it might just float right off his shoulders.

CHAPTER 28

The great thing about an in-service day was the golf team could get out and play 18 holes and not just the usual nine, which meant Bridge Academy's first practice of the season would be a five-hour affair, at least. Only it wasn't just a practice—the guys had already been practicing on their own time.

No, this 18-hole round of golf was more like a try-out, and it would determine the lineup for their first dual match, against Star Christian, the following Tuesday. There would be eight players for five spots and one alternate, which meant two guys wouldn't be making the team.

Max suspected these two unlucky souls would be R.J. Hertzenberg and Deke Rawlins, two guys from the wrestling team who seemed to have signed up to play as a bit of a lark. Both heavyweights, they had finished 1-2, respectively, in the state. But golf? Max didn't even know they played.

It was sunny, about 70 degrees, no wind—and Max, looking at the digital clock in his room, realized he was running late—rolled up a windbreaker and tied it around his waist. He packed a knapsack full of his homework, a book, the family iPad, two sandwiches and a couple of juice boxes, and a windbreaker and some sunscreen for Gabe.

His little brother was Max's one nonnegotiable condition. If Max was going to go back to the job of team manager then not only would Dewey be allowed to play golf with the team at practices and try-outs, but so would Gabe, who looked like he would be a lock to play on the team when he got old enough, anyway.

"Done," Mrs. McQuaid said. "Their tee times are secure. Just send me the bill. Now get out there and win us a state title!"

News of Gabe's eerily perfect swing was spreading. Al Geiberger, or his manager with a stamp of Al Geiberger's autograph, had returned Max's letter about Gabe, saying he was intrigued, and Sadie, using only the iPad, had sent the great man a video file of Gabe (Li'l Geiberger) hitting balls before a small crowd at the Warm Springs range.

Max and Gabe walked to school, where Dewey was waiting outside the big, brown team van. Dewey arched his eyebrows. "What do you know, Coach?"

"Stop calling me that," Max said. "You're the coach. It's your stipend."

Dewey and Gabe piled in along with the five fall team members plus Ed Hocking from New York. (As if to underline their outsider status, Hertzenberg and Rawlins had secured alternate transportation.) Max stowed everyone's clubs in the back behind the swinging doors.

Not until he sat down in the front passenger seat did he realize he'd made a terrible mistake. He had thought he would feel triumphant in his return, but these were still the same five guys sitting behind him who had voted Max Buras off the team in the fall. That part hadn't changed. To them he was still the same loser he'd been before. How had he not anticipated it?

"What's with the pink basket?" Dewey said as he drove the brown van.

Max looked down at the basket, the single dollar bill, and the sign above it on the dashboard: THANK YOU FOR YOUR GENEROUS TIPS.

"Apparently this used to be a hotel shuttle," Max said. "Mr. Raymundo told me. I guess it went to the airport and the Holiday Inn Express, and the school got a good price on it."

"Huh," Dewey said, pulling up to a four-way stop sign. "Thing looks like it got pried off the handlebars of a girl's bike."

Max thought about the team's mutiny in the fall, how he'd felt after the one thing that was right in his life had been so rudely taken away from him—*pried* from his grasp. It was going to be a long 20 minutes before they got to the golf course, way out in Nampa.

No, Max hadn't quite thought this through. Dewey waited their turn and pulled forward, the van picking up speed as it headed for the Interstate.

"Hey, Max."

Max twisted around in his seat, looking back at Hadley Jackson, one of two players who had taken Max's side in the team vote in the fall. (But still the only one whose identity was known.) Hadley sat by the van's left windows. Gabe sat in the emptier third row of seats, way in the back, where he didn't have to touch anyone.

"Yeah," Max said. "Hey, Hadley. What's up?"

It appeared Hadley was trying to grow a goatee, without much success. "We messed up," he said over the center console. "We all did. We blew it."

"It's all right," Max said.

"Aw, it was a crap thing to do," Phil Hendrickson said.

Wait. Was he Max's other defender?

"We just got frustrated, is all," Don Kennerly said.

"Frustrated with the rain," Alex Fisk added. "Five hours in the freezing rain. And all those crappy scores we shot. And Phil losing his 6-iron after shooting 102."

"Thanks for reminding me," Phil said. "Tool."

"We just wanted to man up and tell you as a team," Hadley said. "We know we've been over all of this before. So this is us, saying it as a team."

Max felt a familiar ache in his chest, and his lower lip trembled. No, no, no, he couldn't cry. He absolutely couldn't cry. He had to make a speech, or something.

"We're glad you're, like, our manager and everything," Alex said. "You were always basically the coach, anyway. Mr. Raymundo didn't do anything, anyway. Guy was a terrible golfer, too. So, you know, thanks for stepping up and saving our sorry butts when you did."

Max looked at Alex for an explanation, but none was forthcoming.

"Saving you from what?" Max asked.

No one spoke.

"Saving you from what?" Max asked again.

Hadley leaned forward in the backseat. "You didn't hear?"

"No. What?" Max asked.

"If you and Dewey didn't step up and do this Mrs. McQuaid was going to have to be our coach," Hadley said. "That's what I heard. Have you seen that green visor?"

Laughter rippled through the back of the van.

Suddenly it all made sense, Max and Dewey landing in the principal's office, the random use of educational research to support an even more random personnel decision.

Mrs. McQuaid had been desperate.

Max looked over Alex's shoulder at Pete Whiting and Ed Hocking, who sat on opposite ends of the third row of seats, as far away from each other as possible, looking out their respective side windows.

"We're hitting every green light," Dewey said with a wink.

"I noticed that," Max said. He looked behind him at Gabe in the way back, who was staring out the window at some birds. Apparently *bio-harmonic convergence* worked on traffic signals.

Dewey took a deep breath. "Okay, well," he started, looking in the rearview mirror. "I've been trying to come up with what to say, as your new coach. And what I've come up with—"

"Here comes the speech!" Alex laughed.

"And what I've come up with," Dewey continued, "is this: Go play."

They waited for him to keep going, to expound, to pontificate, but he was done.

"Geez," Alex said. "That's it? I've gotta say, Mr. T, I'm a little disappointed."

"And win one for the Gipper," Dewey said from the driver's seat.

"The Gipper!" Gabe said from between Hadley and Ed Hocking.

"Yeah," Max said, laughing. "Win one for the Gipper."

Dewey turned the van onto the Interstate. "Who is the Gipper, anyway?"

"George Gipp," Ed Hocking said from the way back. "Played football for Notre Dame. Died of strep throat when he was 25."

"He's looking at his phone!" someone said.

"Thanks, Wikipedia," Alex said. "I'm just going to call you Wiki." A few players laughed nervously. "Geez, that's a nice story," Alex added. "A real rib-tickler—let's go win one for the guy with the diseased larynx or whatever."

"You'll be calling me number one, after today," Ed said.

"Whoa!" Alex laughed. "New York State of Mind is feelin' it!"

"Aw, man," Don said. "Who farted?"

"Whoever smelt it, dealt it!"

Max got his clipboard out. "Okay, okay, calm down, we've got 10 today including our visitors from the wrestling team, so it'll be two foursomes and a twosome. Whiting, Hocking, Fisk and Jackson, you're off with the first tee time. And Hendrickson, Kennerly, Hertzenberg and Rawlins, second tee time."

"Oh, man, we got the wrestlers!" Phil said.

"Hey, but if there's any trouble out there…" Alex said.

"Yeah, we could whoop you guys if it comes down to half nelsons," Phil said, finishing the thought. "Oh, man, this is gonna be the longest round of the year."

"It's an open tryout," Max said. "And open means open. And you're not going to be the last ones to the house because Dewey and Gabe will trail behind you guys."

"Little Geiberger!" Alex and Hadley said at the same time, setting off laughter.

Gabe nervously tipped his cap.

❋ ❋ ❋

Max got his homework done in the first hour. He played online Scrabble, using the clubhouse's WiFi for about 20 minutes. The rest of the time he set about learning his lines for his audition to play Phil Connors in *Groundhog Day*, which entailed a lot of murmuring while the girl behind the concession stand regarded him as one regards a lunatic.

Four hours later the results were in. Ed Hocking, it turned out, was not only the most sophisticated player on the team, but he was also, as Max suspected that day on the range, the best. His 3-under-par 69 easily beat the next best Bridge player, Alex Fisk at 74.

"Who won state last year?" Phil asked.

"That kid from Idaho Falls," Max said. "He shot 71."

Pete Whiting, perhaps too keyed up to defend his No. 1 spot in the lineup, came in with a 75; Hadley Jackson had a 78; Phil Hendrickson and Don Kennerly each shot 82; and wrestlers Hertzenberg and Rawlins shot 108 and a 114, respectively, but were just as chipper as ever.

"We were just in it for the free round, man," said Hertzenberg, wearing jeans, a rugby shirt, a dilapidated old cowboy hat and sandals. "Killer course, man. Totally killer."

"Seriously fun," Rawlins added, sliding his Caterpillar cap around to face backward. "That was a blast."

"Oh," Max said. "That's cool. I'm glad you guys had fun."

"Whoa, Mr. T," Hertzenberg said. "You got new teeth!"

"That I did," Dewey said. "Old ones were getting a bit up there in miles."

"Dang, man," Deke said. "Turn those things down! They're hurting my eyes!"

"New York State of Mind!" Alex said. "Nice round, man!"

Alex touched knuckles with Ed Hocking. "Thanks, Alex."

Max felt several pairs of eyes turn to Pete Whiting, whose status as Bridge's No. 1 golfer was fast disappearing over the horizon, but he offered no reaction. The clubhouse concession stand girl was working as fast as she could to load up the team with junk food for the ride back to campus. Gabe had wandered off and was watching a monster truck pull competition on the giant flat-screen TV behind them.

"Hey," Max said, tapping Dewey on the shoulder.

"Hey, Max."

"So how'd it go?"

"Went fine!" Dewey said. "Beautiful day out there."

"What'd you guys shoot? What'd Gabe shoot?"

The question begged to be asked: What kind of scores might come of such a beautiful swing?

"I don't know," Dewey said with a shrug. "We didn't keep score. Were we supposed to?"

Max felt his shoulders slump. "Nah. I was just curious."

What was he expecting? That Gabe would break the course record in his first-ever 18-hole round of golf? That his bio-harmonic convergence with Dewey would translate into a round of 62 or 63?

"I'm just kidding," Dewey said. "I kept score."

"You did?"

"Yeah."

"And?"

"I shot 84," Dewey said.

"No—I mean—I don't care about your score. I mean I do," Max said. "No offense, but I'm wondering what Gabe shot."

Dewey laughed. "I know that. He shot 84, too."

"Oh," Max said. He felt his shoulders slump again.

"Maybe I brought him down," Dewey added. "It's kind of a long course, when you're 10. And he's still getting the hang of putting."

Max looked over at Gabe, who remained entranced by the trucks on the TV screen. "I just thought with the *alchemy* and all, maybe—"

"Maybe today just wasn't the day," Dewey said. "Maybe May 14 will be the day."

"Your birthdays," Max said.

"Our birthdays," Dewey repeated. "And, of course, the state tournament."

CHAPTER TWENTY NINE

CHAPTER

Fireworks. Trumpets. Weightlessness. As Max stood on the stage at the Cathedral of the Rockies, amid a fake ice sculpture and a fake TV news truck and a fake groundhog, he thought of all of these things and none of these things at once. His brain and his heart were throwing off fountains of sparks that lit up the dark and warmed him from within and made him feel tall and tingly.

Was this what was meant by the term *miracle*? He was in a church, after all, and he was kissing Susannah Jurevicious, but wait—was she kissing him back? She was. She was definitely kissing him back.

How long had they been up here? And what were they here for again? Was this even really happening? Yes. It was happening. She smelled like shampoo and tasted like peppermint and wasn't as tall as he'd feared, or maybe he was taller than he'd known and more than he'd dared hope he could be.

He'd gone to the YMCA to lift first—Sadie's suggestion—to get his confidence up and get himself in the proper frame of mind. He'd nearly walked into traffic reading his script one last time on the walk to the church. *I'm just interested in you. What do you want? What do you like? What kind of men are you interested in? What do you do for fun?*

He'd walked through the church doors and checked in with the orange-haired girl—"It's Maxx—double the *X* at the end, if you don't mind. It's my stage name."—and finally he'd waited for all of the various combinations and permutations of Phil and Rita wannabes to take their turns.

But none of these things seemed sufficient to explain how Max Buras was here, now, kissing Susannah Jurevicious amid the warm island breezes and the ukulele music and the drinks with pineapple and—

"Hey! Eminem!"

Max and Susannah unclenched and giggled before looking down at Mrs. Hickenlooper, who had crossed her arms and held a large sheaf of papers in one hand. "What's with all the kissing?"

"Ooh, I think we have our first SHOW-mance!" Lilly Robinson said from somewhere behind Mrs. Hickenlooper, cracking up pretty much the entire church full of prospective cast members.

Max, whom his math teacher had been calling Eminem since he'd correctly guessed the exact number of candies in her glass jar, recognized Sadie's laugh but couldn't see her.

His face felt red. He didn't care.

"You guys are way ahead of yourselves," Mrs. Hickenlooper said. "This isn't even the ice sculpture scene yet." She looked down at her papers. "You're in the Tip Top Diner.

"Rita: *I guess I want what everybody wants—you know, career, love, marriage, children.*

"Phil: *Are you seeing anyone?*

"Rita: *I think this is getting too personal.*

"Right? Is this ringing any bells?"

"Yeah, we know that," Susannah said. "We just thought we'd get it out of the way, the kissing part, just so we wouldn't be thinking about it the whole time we were up here."

"Right," Max said, except he knew he would be thinking about kissing Susannah Jurevicious for the rest of his life.

He'd been all set to read his lines opposite Lilly Robinson when Susannah all but body-blocked Lilly off the stage, giving Max his first indication that maybe her instructions to "*call me sometime*" hadn't been a throwaway line at all.

They'd fumbled a little with their scripts until he'd gotten them started with, *No matter what happens tomorrow, or for the rest of my life, I'm happy now because I love you.* And she'd said, *I think I'm happy, too.* And then he'd kissed Susannah Jurevicious, changing his life forever.

"It's like Susannah said," he said, addressing Mrs. Hickenlooper, who was tapping her foot and looking at her watch. "We just wanted to, um, workshop the ice sculpture scene at the end, just to, you know—"

"Well, why do we even have scripts?" Mrs. Hickenlooper tossed her papers up into the air and Max watched as they fell into a mess at her feet. "Let's just make it up as we go along!"

The church got very quiet.

"Okay," Susannah said. Max fought back a laugh.

"Freddy!" Mrs. Hickenlooper said. "Come pick up my script!"

Freddy Robinson, who was reading for the part of Ned Ryerson, scurried around at Mrs. Hickenlooper's feet, gathering up the strewn papers.

"Here," Susannah whispered, handing Max an Altoid. "I think we have to do as she says and go back to the diner scene. But keep this for later, not that you need it. I want some more practice." She nudged him in the ribs.

In his mind, Max heard the echo of Andy Hastings. *Whoa.*

☀ ☀ ☀

Conrad Stapleton won the part of Phil Connors, and this was because, Mrs. Hickenlooper said, he had "superior comic timing." Max didn't much care. He hadn't been able to remember his lines, anyway, what with his brain having turned to goo amid all that kissing, and he figured anyone named Conrad Stapleton had better have a sense of humor, and good for him.

Also, Susannah Jurevicious hadn't won her part, either, which may have been because she was better at volleyball than acting. She kept coming down with the case of the giggles every time she had to deliver a line, and Max assumed it had been a fairly easy choice for Mrs. Hickenlooper to fill the Rita role with Lilly Robinson, a proven talent in the Bridge theater arts community.

(Also, it probably hadn't hurt that she was also an administrative assistant to Mrs. McQuaid, giving Mrs. Hickenlooper a direct line to the principal if the production ever needed some assistance from on high.)

Sadie got the role of Phil Connors's piano teacher, which she seemed happy about.

Max and Susannah were offered positions as stagehands, which was no small job as it involved a great deal of fake snow, a news van, an endless supply of plates and mugs to be smashed to bits on the Tip Top Diner floor, and the animatronic groundhog that Lilly and Freddy Robinson's mother had found on the Internet.

Max and Susannah declined, but kept right on practicing the ice sculpture scene on their own at his house, her house and at the movies, and once in an unlit exit at school when no one was looking.

"If you two ever have kids," Sadie said with a sigh one night, "I hope for the sake of poetic justice you name them Phil and Rita."

"Or Conrad and Lilly," Max said, "in honor of our esteemed colleagues who actually got the roles."

For some reason this sent Susannah off into a fit of giggles, and Max couldn't imagine a sweeter sound. For such a killer on the volleyball court, she sure liked to laugh.

Dewey sometimes kidded Max about his new girlfriend, and they compared notes like a couple of old married men, Dewey besotted with "talk doc" Cynthia and Max head over heels over Susannah. Gabe had become unreasonably attached to his white newsboy cap, removing it only for showering and bedtime.

Life was good.

Bridge crushed Star Christian in the first dual meet of the season, won an invitational the week after that, and then waltzed to easy victories in two more dual meets.

The addition of Ed Hocking to what was already a strong team was proving to make for a formidable squad. New York State of Mind, as Alex called him, had already shot two 70s, a 72 and a 73. The Bridge lineup, one to six, had pretty much sorted itself out as Hocking, Whiting, Fisk, Kennerly, Hendrickson and Hadley Jackson, whose swing had gotten all mixed up after getting an unsolicited tip from Pete Whiting's dad up at the club, and who was now fighting a horrible slice and switching out his driver for a different one every other round.

Not that it mattered, since their scores didn't count, but Gabe and Dewey kept bringing up the rear and shooting the exact same score. It came as no surprise to Max, what with their matching birthdays and die-cast tie fighters and bio-harmonic convergence, but some of the guys on the team had begun to notice. Gabe and Dewey's best was two 80s; their worst, 89s.

Gabe was the same either way, just happy to tag along and be part of it all.

It wasn't until the end of April that Max began to hear the rumors, and within a matter of days the ugly rumors hardened into terrible facts.

Dewey's background check, which had initially come back clean, hadn't given a "full and honest accounting" of the black sheep.

CHAPTER 30

Max sat in his chair and knew without a sliver of doubt: This was some kind of record, his fourth trip to the principal's office in one year.

Not that he was happy about it. The last 24 hours in the Buras home had been fraught with tears and misunderstandings and long explanations.

"I wanted to tell you guys," Dewey had said, sitting on the living room couch and wiping his eyes and nose with his fourth or fifth Kleenex. He'd started smoking again, and Cynthia was threatening to leave him.

"It was complicated," he said to the ground, head in his hands. "It is complicated. It's complicated."

It had been the family meeting to end all family meetings, absent Sadie and Gabe, whom Max's parents had sent to Dave & Buster's with unlimited quarters out of the "Trip to Hawaii" jar that sat next to the phone in the kitchen. Dewey had explained everything, how he'd come to kill a man in Seattle with his bare hands, under a bridge, as night fell.

And now, here in Mrs. McQuaid's office, in the presence of the school principal, Max, Max's parents, and some guy Max had never seen before, Dewey was going to have to explain it all again.

"Thank you all for coming," Mrs. McQuaid said, looking out at her rather large audience, her gaze stopping on the unidentified man in a suit. "This is Mr. Johnson," she said, "legal counsel for the school district."

The guy in the suit got up and shook hands all around. He had smooth, cold hands, with shiny fingernails.

Mrs. McQuaid turned to Dewey. "I see you've chosen not to bring legal counsel, which is your prerogative. Mr. and Mrs. Buras, Max, Dwight, as you know we've been treating this as an internal matter."

"Oh, I appreciate that," Dewey said. "I truly do."

"But I'm afraid I'm going to need to hear your side," she said.

"Right," he said. He worked his hands, studied his nails. Max tried to find his breath—so much for easing into things. Dewey began: "The thing is, I've gotta ask you, how thorough a background check did you do? Because normally, see, you might get a guy who says he hopes you weren't *too* thorough with him. Now I, on the other—"

"It says here you killed a man," Mrs. McQuaid said. She leaned forward in her chair, looked down at something on her desk. "At a gathering place for the homeless called Hobo Hangout, in Washington State, June 15, 1998. You didn't think this might be worth mentioning on the form, where it asks if you've ever been convicted of a crime?"

"I was exonerated," Dewey said.

"Convicted," said Mr. Johnson, the lawyer. "You weren't exonerated until years later."

Dewey said nothing.

"You killed a—"

Max was glad Mr. Johnson didn't get a chance to say it again. He was interrupted as the door to the office swung open and Lilly Robinson—administrative assistant, Rita in *Groundhog Day*—stopped cold.

"Sorry! I didn't know anyone was in here!"

Mrs. McQuaid leaned back in her chair. "Hello, Lilly."

"Hi!"

"Can we help you?"

Lilly cracked her chewing gum. "Oh! Totally. Do we have any duct tape? The door to the groundhog house fell off and Mrs. Hickenlooper says we ran out, and to ask you."

"Lilly," Mrs. McQuaid said.

"Yeah?"

"Please close the door."

"Oh. Totally. Sorry!"

The door closed, and Mrs. McQuaid got up and locked it and sat back down again. "My administrative assistant. I apologize. I thought it was locked.

Dwight, you may continue."

"I don't know what to say," Dewey said. "Your information is correct. But that's not the whole story. If you'd done a thorough investigation—"

"We DID do a thorough investigation," Mrs. McQuaid said.

"We are well aware of the facts," Mr. Johnson said.

"Then you'll know it wasn't his fault," Max's father said. "You'll know it was self-defense and the man was mentally ill and the Northwest Innocence Project uses it as one of their signature victories of the last 20 years. You'll know that Dewey's original lawyer was disbarred."

Max had never felt such admiration for his father.

"Put that in your file," Harold Buras added.

"It's already there," Mrs. McQuaid said. "And we're going to need to hear it from Dwight. That's why we're all here today, to hear his side of the story without the lawyers. No offense."

"None taken," Mr. Johnson said.

"I'm gonna need a cigarette," Dewey said.

"Why don't you just start from the beginning," Mrs. McQuaid said.

"Just tell them like you told us," Max's mother said before blowing her nose into a tissue. She laughed. "I'm sorry," she said, shaking her head. "This is all a bit much."

"Bedding," Dewey said.

Max looked at his feet. This was the most unbelievable part.

"Excuse me? I thought you said 'bedding,'" Mrs. McQuaid said.

"I did," Dewey said. "You said start at the beginning, and bedding is the beginning. Hobo Hangout is a place where a lot of people sleep, and it was where I slept, at that point in my life, along with a whole lot of others."

"We're aware of that, yes," Mr. Johnson said. His legs were crossed, and he was looking down at an open, leather-clad binder in his lap.

"So, yeah," Dewey said. "Bedding. I was laying out my sleeping bag for the night, and that's when the guy bum-rushed me."

"This would be—" The suit looked down at his fancy binder. "—one Turk Watson Ford. He rushed you. Or he *bum*-rushed you, excuse me."

"Sorry," Dewey said. "Dumb phrase. But yeah, Turk was the one and he had this crazy look in his eyes and he—then things went from there. I've regretted it ever since."

"You strangled him," Mrs. McQuaid said. "With your bare hands."

"Was either him or me," Dewey said. "He had a knife. I didn't. Kind of a pertinent fact, don't you think?" His foot was tapping the floor, his eyes dancing all over the place in his head. "I'm sorry, can I get that cigarette?"

"And according to the report," Mrs. McQuaid said, "Mr. Ford had a long history of mental illness, but you wound up in Walla-Walla, anyway."

"The Walls," Dewey said, a faraway look in his eyes. "A gated community."

No one laughed.

"But in hindsight you lost in court because your first lawyer was incompetent," Mrs. McQuaid said, consulting her notes. "And then enter the Innocence Project."

"Right. And then enter my second lawyer," Dewey said. "Only took eight years to get to that point, two more after that to get back out on the bricks."

"I'm sorry," the suit said. "But what did bedding have to do with it again?"

"Second lawyer started asking around," Dewey said. "He talked to a lot of the guys who were there that night, at least the ones who were still on the right side of the grass. He found Turk's old right hand, guy named Apples. I don't know what his real name was. Anyway, Apples tells my new guy Turk thought I had his sleeping bag."

"Bedding," Mrs. McQuaid said.

"Bedding," Dewey said. "I guess they looked the same. I don't remember."

"All of this," Mr. Johnson said, "was over a sleeping bag."

Dewey looked at his feet. "Yes," he said, without looking up.

"And after 10 years," Mr. Johnson continued, looking down at his lap, "you're acquitted and sent back out into society and vocational school and here we are."

"Here we are," Max said, surprising himself.

"I'm going to fight this for the rest of my life," Dewey said.

"Yes and no," Mr. Johnson said. "As you started to say before, your best defense is a thorough background check. You're going to want employers to go all the way through to 10 years down the line, and to contact the Innocence Project, and interview you in person. It's only if they stop at the initial rush to judgment that you're in trouble."

The lawyer flashed him a smile and looked back down at his notes. "And what about your record prior to the events of June 15, 1998?"

Dewey smiled, showing his megawatt new teeth. "My misspent youth." He shrugged. "What can I say?"

"Look, he was acquitted," Max's father said, leaning forward in his seat. "I hope you're not going to hold it against him that he switched some price tags around at Target when he was 11! My brothers and I did worse, for heaven's sake. Boys will be boys."

Max wondered exactly what laws his father and uncles had broken back in the day. He'd definitely have to hear that story.

"You should see what Dewey has done for Gabe," Max's mother said.

"He threw himself in front of traffic!" Max said.

"Calm down, everyone," Mrs. McQuaid said. "I'm well aware of what Dwight has done for Gabe. It's a remarkable story."

"It IS remarkable," Max's dad said.

"And because of that, and because of the extenuating circumstances in this case, Mr. Johnson and I are going to present this to the school board, in closed session, before making a final decision."

Mrs. McQuaid stood up and steepled her hands.

"So I've still got a job," Dewey said.

"You've still got a job," Mrs. McQuaid said. "For now."

"He's got *lots* of jobs," Max said, placing his hands on an invisible steering wheel and looking at Mrs. McQuaid to make sure she understood the reference.

If Dewey were to be fired there would be no one left to drive the golf team van. He was the duct tape that held everything together—the family, Gabe, the team. Max wondered if he should call a team meeting and ask Dewey to spill it all, just get it all out in the open. Sunlight, Max's father always said, was the best disinfectant. And it would preclude someone spilling it for him. Max decided he would tell the team, only the team.

CHAPTER

The weeks that led up to the state tournament were marked by the further decline of Hadley Jackson, who now, in the throes of what he described as the worst slump of his career, had decided to forgo the driver altogether in favor of a succession of 3-woods and utility clubs and long irons off the tee. His swing was in shambles, and his psyche had followed. He was a complete wreck.

Other than that, though, the team was showing few weaknesses. Ed Hocking had the best stroke average in the state, and Max's father had sent a cub reporter to write a story about him in the paper. Ed and Pete had even begun spurring each other to shoot lower and lower scores.

Late one Sunday afternoon Max took Gabe out for nine holes at Warm Springs, just to see what would happen when his brother left the nest of Dwight (Dewey) Tomlinson. Max was pleasantly surprised when Gabe shot a 2-over-par 38, an improvement over his usual scores when playing with Uncle Dewey. Max had a 51.

Susannah and Max studied Spanish together—Mr. Raymundo had been especially lenient in grading Max's papers, which didn't feel quite right. They also hung out at the YMCA together and watched old movies on her iPad together. They were going on a month now, and she said that was approaching a personal record, and Max did not say that he'd broken his own personal record upon their first kiss.

Sadie said she might just take up the piano after she was done playing a piano teacher on stage, and Dewey had announced he was going to finally do it, he had found a guide to take him up into the Grand Tetons in July. The school board seemed to be taking its sweet time in deciding his case; they'd be ruling one way or the other any day now.

Most of the talk in the Buras household had turned to what Dewey and Gabe wanted for their birthdays, and Max's parents told him they'd already sprung for an REI gift card and the complete boxed set of Star Wars movies, respectively.

Max found himself preoccupied with the state tournament, which would be held at Hillcrest Country Club the same day. That this was the same course where the team had crashed at districts in the fall was lost on no one, but with a new ace in Ed Hocking it seemed like fate was smiling upon them. Also, there was no chance of snow in the forecast. All signs pointed to a bio-harmonic convergence the likes of which no one had ever seen.

And then it all blew up into a million pieces.

CHAPTER

32

The morning of May 14 may as well have been Christmas. Dewey came over for breakfast, and he and Gabe unwrapped presents. Dewey brought everyone outside and pulled a gleaming, red bicycle out of the back of the old police cruiser.

"I didn't have time to wrap it," he said.

"Whoa," Gabe said.

"Gabe!" Max said. "This is the year you learn to ride a bike!"

"Amazing," Max's dad said. "That is a gorgeous ride, Gabe."

They all went back inside and sat down to a breakfast of eggs and bacon. Gabe ate a few bites before delving into a giant box of Star Wars-themed LEGOs, dumping all 3,152 bricks on the living room floor. Dewey, who had lapsed on his smoking ban, unwrapped a giant box of bubble gum.

"That's from me," Max said. "In case you want to quit again."

"Thanks," Dewey said. He took a sip of coffee. "Big day today!"

"The biggest," Max said. "Butterflies."

"Me, too," Dewey admitted. "Wish I could play for you guys, not that I'd shoot low enough to help the team."

Sadie sat on the living room carpet with Gabe, and they both held up the box with its picture of the LEGO Star Wars Super Star Destroyer.

"I've got to get going," Max's dad said, clearing his plate. "Great gift, Dewey. I'd be there today but I've got a piece due on BSU spring football. We'll have our prep guy there, though. Good luck. I'm sure you guys will rock it."

"Thanks," Max said.

"I'm gonna get going as well," Dewey said. "I said I'd cover the morning rush at the Y. Those old, retired dudes are messier than you'd think. Their aim isn't so good anymore, or maybe it's a stream issue. I don't know."

"Ew. Dewey!"

"Sorry, Sadie." Dewey got up to go.

"Here's this," Max's father said from the doorway on his way out of the house. He reared back with an underhand toss and the wrapped-up newspaper in its clear plastic bag soared across the room and landed on the dining room table.

"Every day the kid throws it in the middle of the sprinklers," his father added. "But today? He lands it smack dab in the middle of the welcome mat. Isn't that something?" He looked at Dewey and Gabe. "See you guys tonight. Good luck this afternoon."

"Keep it—I'll read the copy at the Y," Dewey said, throwing a purple windbreaker over his shoulders and nodding at the morning paper on the table. "Guys leave pieces of the paper all over the place, mostly the sauna. All the news that's fit to soak up sweat!"

❉ ❉ ❉

The news wasn't fit for anything. It wasn't even close. Because on page 3 of the Sports Section, spread open on the kitchen table, was a paid announcement that curdled the eggs in Max's stomach. The headline: "The Murderer in Our School."

There were two photos of Dewey, one that had been taken recently, which Max assumed had come off his badge at the YMCA, and one that was part of a *Seattle Post-Intelligencer* article dated June 16, 1998: "Man held for questioning in death of transient at Hobo Hangout." The article had been photocopied into the paid announcement, and it detailed how Dwight "Dewey" Tomlinson had been arrested and booked and, according to eyewitnesses, had committed murder in the first degree.

There was no mention of the Northwest Innocence Project, or his incompetent first lawyer. Whoever had paid for the announcement in the paper seemed to have decided Dewey was a menace to society.

"Sadie," Max said. "Come here."

"Just a second, we've almost got a wing built."

"Thruster," Gabe said.

"A thruster," Sadie said.

"Just come over here," Max said.

Sadie must have heard it in his voice, because she came over immediately. She was still holding one of the LEGO bricks when she pulled up next to Max and leaned on the kitchen table with her hands. "Oh," she said. "Oh, no. Did Dad know anything about this?"

"I doubt it," Max said. "He'd have said something."

She began to read the paid commentary:

"Bridge Academy has gone a step too far with its so-called 'progressive' educational approach, hiring convicted murderer Dwight 'Dewey' Tomlinson to clean the bathrooms and coach the golf team."

"Oh, man," Max said.

"This is sick," Sadie said.

Max looked down at his sister's hands, which were still holding the white LEGO brick and moving it back and forth now, one hand to the other, her fingers squeezing the factory-milled corners and edges and interlocking nubs.

They read in silence now: three paragraphs that called the school "woefully irresponsible" and "negligent in its failure to apply background checks." There was even mention of Max coaching the golf team with Dewey, which the writer of the paid commentary had called, "the inmates running the asylum."

"This is a paid commentary," Sadie said, still furiously working the LEGO brick in her hands. "This isn't a news article. No one from the paper wrote this, none of Dad's co-workers. So who paid to put this garbage in the paper? Who would do this?"

Max looked down at the bottom-right corner of the page: PAID FOR BY ABC REAL ESTATE, ALAN WHITING, TREASURER.

A red drip fell from on high and landed with a splat in the "A" in "ALAN," and Max looked down at Sadie's red-smudged fingers, her white LEGO brick smeared with blood.

"Sadie," he said. "Your hands. You're bleeding."

❈ ❈ ❈

Dewey was cleaning the sauna when he found it. *Hey, that guy looks like me!* Then he looked closer at the browning, sweat-stained newsprint and realized it really was him. He recognized both pictures. He looked at the two enormous, hairy sweaty guys sitting on the bench, each of them in a wrapped up towel, each with his eyes closed, oblivious.

There was no need to read the fine print; the headline said it all. He could guess the rest. He stormed out of the sauna, dropped his nametag in the trash on the way out, and found the Crown Vic parked on State Street, pointed west. The sun was shining as if no one had told it that someone's life just ended, and Dewey turned the ignition and headed for the Grandview Motel.

There wasn't much traffic at this hour, 10:05 a.m., but he hit every red light. His room was just as he'd left it: bed unmade, some dirty clothes on the floor, an empty pizza box, and a giant felt Gru head sitting in the corner from Halloween. The place smelled like pepperoni.

He had always made it a point not to collect *stuff*, which made it easier to never get caught with more possessions than would fit in a suitcase for a fast getaway. There was no need for a fast getaway now, no one was coming to get him, but then again there was no reason to stay, either. Not now. He scooped up some change on his bedside table, and there it was, the familiar card of the woman who looked like Cleopatra, *Madam Hagar: Psychic Medium for Apparitions, Poltergeists, and all things Paranormal.*

"You batty old loony-toon," he said.

This was what it had all come down to? All of that airy-fairy talk of bio-harmonic convergence and Max and Gabe and video poker and speech therapy and golf—and for what? To what end? Dewey dialed the number.

"This number is no longer in service. If you feel you have reached this number in error, please hang—"

It was satisfying, in its way, watching his phone shatter against the mirror at that speed. The impact blew up both instantly, and Dewey felt a pang of regret—How would Cynthia reach him now? How would Gabe? How would Max? And how much would he have to pay to replace that crappy mirror? But a few seconds went by, and the throw felt worth all that. No one would want to talk to him anymore, anyway. There was no reason to call a dead man.

He tossed three armfuls worth of gear in the trunk, went back for one last look around his boxy home, and didn't bother to latch the door closed on the way out.

❀ ❀ ❀

"Thanks for meeting me on such short notice. This is an impressive turnout for a Saturday morning. We're all busy people, and I know you all have things to do."

Sadie was going to enjoy this. Max was readying the golf team, or what was left of it, so somebody had to do what needed to be done, and she hadn't given it a second thought. She'd always been a good organizer. She looked up from her bandaged finger at R.J. Hertzenberg, Deke Rawlins, Hadley Jackson, Graham Godwin and Freddy and Lilly Robinson. They were gathered just off the greenbelt, between the asphalt and the rushing water, about a 10 minute walk from the school. The river was running high. It was 11:53 a.m. Dewey was apparently quite a bit more popular than the school's last janitor, who never smiled and was finally fired for drinking on the job.

"I don't have anything to do," R.J. said. "Wrestling season is over."

"Yeah, me, neither," Deke said.

"And this was a sucker punch," R.J. said. "It demands a response."

"Yeah," Deke said. "D.T. probably never even saw it coming."

Sadie stepped off the greenbelt to make way for a pair of cyclists, all decked out in their compression shorts and team shirts—GEORGE'S BICYCLES—with all of their pouches. "G'morning," one of them said as he whizzed past them.

None of them responded in kind. Not for Dewey Tomlinson it wasn't a good morning, and with any luck it wasn't going to be so good for Alan Whiting, either.

"Okay, well, this is gonna be big," Sadie continued, "and we could get in trouble, so if any of you want to back out now, speak now or forever try to get it off your permanent record. And whatever you do, Max can't know about this. He would love to be here, but he's the coach and it would put him in a bad spot to even hear about it.

"When I give the word we're going to walk over to that office park over there." She pointed at a vast parking lot that began about a 20 yards from the river. "And we are going to lock onto our target in the parking lot. Our target will be parked just outside ABC Real Estate, which is located directly between the Cottonwood Grill and Happy Home Title Company. Our target is a Lexus SUV belonging to one Alan Whiting. It has an American flag decal and the following words: *2022 U.S. Open at The Country Club in Brookline, Massachusetts*."

Freddy raised his hand.

"Yes, Freddy? You don't have to raise your hand."

"What's *ABC* stand for?"

"Always Be Closing," someone said, and Sadie whirled around to face Pete Whiting. He was wearing a pair of new looking chinos, a Nike golf shirt and a pair of white FootJoy shoes with plastic spikes, as if he had a tee time later, which he did.

"Don't even bother," Sadie said. "Our mind's already made up, and if you haven't noticed, you're badly outnumbered."

Deke and R.J. took two steps toward him.

"I'm not here to stop you," Pete said. "I'm here to help you."

Sadie scrunched up her face. "You are?"

"Yeah."

"Why?"

Pete stuck his hands in his pockets and looked out at the river, then back at the parking lot and finally at Sadie again. "Because I hate that car," he said.

Sadie smiled. "Okay, then. Who brought the eggs?"

No one spoke.

"No one brought the eggs?"

"I didn't know we were supposed to," Lilly Robinson said. "You should have specified that in the text!"

"We don't need eggs," Deke said. "We'll roll it."

"Roll it where?" Hadley said.

Deke looked at the river and smiled.

"Wait," Sadie said. Egging a car was one thing, but dumping it in the river, totally wrecking it, was another. It wasn't the type of thing an adult easily forgave; it could go on her permanent record. But then she heard the words of R.J., or maybe it was Deke, who had said once that *anything worth doing is worth overdoing*, or maybe she'd just heard it on TV. "Pete," she said to the late arrival, "do you have a key to your dad's car? Because that would be a whole lot easier than what we're planning on here."

"No, he hides that stuff." Pete looked out at the river again.

It was, Sadie would recall later, surprisingly easy to cartwheel a car into the river. Deke and R.J. and Pete, varsity athletes all, might have been strong enough to get it done on their own, but they had more manpower than that—eight of them in all.

They grunted and heaved and rolled the car over on its side, the windows crunching to bits, and then rolling it onto its roof, and then onto its other side, smashing the rest of the windows. They rolled it up over a curb and onto some grass, taking up great big chunks of turf, and over the greenbelt as a few cyclists stopped to watch.

"It's okay," Lilly said. "Science experiment. Displacement! H2O!"

The cyclists nodded stupidly. Sadie couldn't imagine they believed it, though, because with each mighty shove, Pete Whiting kept saying, "There's no YOU in team! There's no YOU in team!" His cheeks were wet; he seemed to be crying.

He said it like that all the way until they watched the crumpled Lexus roll down the embankment, over a few overmatched, scrubby trees, and into the fast-moving water. "THERE. IS. NO. YOU. IN. TEAM!!!!" Pete's screams drowned out the sound of breaking branches as the car toppled into the river and hit the water with a tremendous splash.

They stood on the bank and watched the SUV bob to the surface of the river before slowly making its way downriver, twisting and turning.

"Thanks for the golf lesson," Hadley Jackson said softly. "Jerk."

The car disappeared from view as the eight of them stood on the bank in silent reverence.

In his corner office overlooking the parking lot, Alan Whiting was lost in thought, his head in his computer, a college golf recruiting website up on the screen. He imagined a future in which he attended very important golf tournaments, undoubtedly as a VIP guest of his son, as his U.S. Open car bobbed and floated under the Americana Boulevard Bridge, skirted a fisherman, spooked some trout, and slowly made its way toward Oregon.

✿ ✿ ✿

By the end of the golf season the van smelled of socks and cheese.

Max sat in the passenger seat, his mind racing as they poked along in light traffic on their way to the golf course for the state tournament. They hit a lot of red lights.

The day that had begun with so much promise had curdled in the time it takes to read a hateful newspaper article, and the team was already showing early signs of disintegration. Gabe was there but Dewey was not. And there was no telling what had happened to Bridge's second-best golfer, Pete Whiting, or the struggling No. 5 man Hadley Jackson. They would have to make their own way to the course.

"Thanks for driving," Max said.

Mr. Raymundo looked across the center console and smiled. "*No te preocupes.*"

"What?"

"Don't worry about it. The least I could do. I'm sorry about what happened in the fall. *Lo siento.*"

They pulled up to a red light, the van's brakes groaning and creaking.

"I guess everybody has a bad day," Max said.

Mr. Raymundo looked at him for an extra beat. "Did you do something to your hair? You look different."

Max smiled. The guy had always been a flake—he passed out quizzes and told them not to cheat and then inexplicably left the room for up to a half hour at a time. But Max didn't know he was quite this much of a space cadet. "I got rid of my glasses," he said. "I got the LASIK surgery. And I've been working out, and eating better. And I grew four inches."

Mr. Raymundo banged the steering wheel with his palm and leaned back in his seat. "The glasses."

They both looked back out onto the mostly empty road, and Max tried to imagine where Dewey might be, where he'd been when he saw the paid message on Page 3 of the Sports Section that morning, if he'd seen it. He was probably at the Y, spraying the machines down with disinfectant.

The guys were quiet in the back of the van, even Alex. They seemed to sense something was up, although how many of them had seen the paid notice in the paper was impossible to say, and Max certainly wasn't about to bring it up. They had a tournament to play.

Gabe was sitting between Phil Hendrickson and Ed Hocking, softly humming and moaning as he rocked forward and backward in his seat and looking around for the missing Dewey.

"Hang in there, little brother," Max said.

The van pulled into the parking lot. Although Max had held out hope that Pete and Hadley and Dewey would be at the course when the van arrived, they were not. Forty minutes remained until the first tee time, the top four seeds in the state, a foursome that would include Bridge's Ed Hocking, but then things would get tricky.

Pete was in a tee time with the No. 2s, 24 minutes later, and while it would be another hour-plus before the No. 5s went off, Hadley's absence was worrisome, too, since Bridge Academy would require a minimum of four signed scorecards in order to not be disqualified. If Pete didn't make his tee time, then Hadley's score was going to count no matter how bad he was playing. If he showed up.

The team filed out of the van and onto the driving range to warm up. Max knew he should eat something. He hadn't managed to get down much of his mom's egg dish before finding the appetite-souring paid message from Alan Whiting in the paper, but his stomach was still too jumpy. He had just exited the pro shop when he spotted a gangly, kind-faced old man in a light beige cardigan and finely creased khaki slacks and a pair of loafers.

The man was too old to be a coach; Max decided the guy must be someone's grandpa. Whoever he was, he was walking a straight line toward Max. "Are you Max?" the man said.

Max stopped, looked up, and recognized the man from his instructional video.

"Al Geiberger," the man said, offering his hand. He had lines around his face, and was slightly stooped at the waist.

"I—uh, hi," Max said. Al Geiberger's hand was as rough as sandpaper;

how many golf balls he must have hit, how much time spent toiling on driving ranges around the world.

"You came," Max said. "I didn't think you'd come."

Al Geiberger smiled, eyes twinkling. "Of course! I wouldn't miss it. Thanks for reaching out. It's not every day I see my old golf swing in miniature. I don't even see my old swing in the mirror anymore! Although to be fair, I don't get out much. I'm not a young man anymore."

"You know he doesn't play," Max said. "I mean he plays, but he'll just bring up the rear behind the others. His score doesn't count. He's too young." Max wondered whom Gabe was going to play *with*, what with Dewey having gone missing.

"Oh, I don't care about all that," Al Geiberger said. "I just want to see him! Is he out on the range now?"

"He is. Look for the little guy in a white cap with your swing."

"That's wonderful. I will. Good luck to you. Good luck to Bridge."

"Thanks," Max said.

They were going to need it.

Max made his way over to the practice putting green, where Ed Hocking was methodically going through his drills. Mr. Raymundo stood with his arms crossed in front of his chest, taking in the view of the Boise treetops. He turned to Max.

"Did you bring your clubs?"

"No. Gawd no. And even if I did, there's no way—"

"You can use mine," Mr. Raymundo said. "They're going to need your score. Can Gabe play?"

"What? He's only 10! I mean, he's only 11! And he's already on edge with Dewey not here. There's no way—"

"He's gonna need to go out there," Mr. Raymundo said, looking at his watch. "I don't think those other guys are coming. He's your best bet to go in for Whiting in the No. 2 group. You need to tell the coaches."

Max's stomach squawked. "Can he even play in this thing? Is he eligible? I thought he was too young."

"I don't know," Mr. Raymundo said. "He goes to Bridge, right? Let me talk to the other coaches. I think they'll let it slide. That okay?"

"Go ahead," Max said, looking at his watch. "Where are your clubs?"

"Ah, yes. They're over there in the Corona bag. It was a freebie. You like TaylorMade?"

"I don't know if it makes a difference," Max said, rolling his neck and bending from the waist. "I guess we don't have a choice. I've got to play."

Max shouldered Mr. Raymundo's Corona bag and made his way over to the range, where he pulled up next to Al Geiberger behind tiny Gabe. He was hitting balls with his perfect little swing amid all the bigger boys, already with their game faces on. Gabe didn't deserve this. He wasn't ready for this. All he wanted was to be with Dewey.

"Gabe," Max said, his hands on his knees to get down to eye level. One of Mr. Raymundo's clubs, which were still strapped onto Max's back, fell out of the Corona bag and onto the ground.

His brother stopped hitting balls.

Max continued: "You're going to play with the big boys today, okay?"

Gabe's eyes got wide. "Dewey."

"No Dewey—the big boys, Gabe, the boys," Max repeated, nodding at the kids up and down the tee line. "No bogeys today, okay?"

Gabe looked back at his pile of range balls.

"Yeah," he said. "No bogeys. No Dewey."

Max wanted to hug his brother, to protect him from whatever was about to happen.

He went to find an open stall to hit balls, his stomach knotted full of dread.

❧ ❧ ❧

There was no miracle. Playing in the No. 5 group for Bridge, with clubs that were not his own, Max shot a 102 and tried on every shot. It was not a good score, but not so terrible as to attract much notice. The others in the group had most likely just thought he'd had a bad day.

Mr. Raymundo, who had taken over for Max in announcing the players on the first tee, patted him on the shoulders. "You did your best," he said. "Maybe it was my clubs. Feel free to blame the clubs, *amigo*."

"It wasn't the clubs," Max said.

They were in the clubhouse, the players milling around under the big paper scoreboard while the coaches added up the numbers. Max was still in a daze when he saw Gabe in the corner of the room, walking in circles and moaning. Max ran to his brother, but their mother came barging through the clubhouse doors and went straight to him, getting there first and wrapping him up in a hug before Gabe elbowed her off him.

There was mud on his pants, and his hair was mussed, his face slicked with sweat. His eyes had a feral, faraway look, and he seemed to have lost his white newsboy cap.

"Oh, man, Gabe," Max said. "Come back to us, buddy."

"I've got him," their mother said. "Go do your job. Go be the coach."

Gabe began another big arc around the perimeter of the room as Max pulled away and looked up at the scores, written in thick black and red ink.

Hocking: 65.

Whoa.

Fisk: 74.

Not bad. At this rate they had a shot at it. He scanned the list of names but the calligrapher hadn't posted any of the other Bridge scores. Hocking's score, Max would later find out, was the lowest anyone had shot in the state tournament in almost 20 years.

Al Geiberger was standing in the middle of the room signing autographs and Max sidled up alongside. "Excuse me, Mr. Geiberger?"

"Well hello, Max. How'd it go out there?"

"For me? Oh, well, I'm not much of a golfer. How did Gabe do?"

The calligrapher hadn't posted his score, and Gabe looked like he'd retreated too far into himself again to offer any kind of report on his round.

"Oh, he was splendid, just splendid," Geiberger said. "For 17 holes. I've never seen anything like it. What a swing! I never could have imagined when I made the video that it would take root in such a profound—"

"What do you mean, 'For 17 holes'?"

Max could see Gabe was spinning around in place in the corner of the clubhouse, their mother looking on helplessly.

"He was three over par through 17 holes," Geiberger said. "Which for a player that size is remarkable. Did you know that little guy can't even reach some of the par-4s in two? What a marvelous short game."

Geiberger smiled to reveal a complicated set of dental replacements, much like Dewey's.

"I know, I know," Max said. "Then what happened?"

The calligrapher posted another Bridge score: Kennerly 78. Wow. This was going well. As long as Gabe posted a score and they didn't have to use Max's ghastly 102, Bridge might win.

"Then he got to 18," Geiberger said. "Did you know there's a glider port on 18? Just off the fairway there?"

"Oh," Max said. His heart sank. "Well—so he got distracted," he said hopefully. "That's no big deal. It happens to us all. So what'd he make on the hole? A bogey? Double-bogey?"

"He didn't," Geiberger said.

"He didn't what?"

"He didn't make a score. He didn't finish the hole. I think he liked watching the gliders more than he liked playing golf. I think they pleased him." Geiberger smiled.

"They pleased him," Max repeated.

"They amused him. He took out a little plane out of his golf bag. It had six-sided wings. He made it climb and swoop just the way the gliders were. And when it was his turn to hit, from the middle of the fairway, he was—well, he was no longer even on the course. He'd wandered over to the glider port."

"So you're saying he didn't post a score," Max said, his vision suddenly failing him again amid a dizzying kaleidoscope of fractals.

"I'm afraid not," Geiberger said.

"Did anyone try to snap him out of it? Did anyone go to help him? He's only 10, for God's sakes! He's only 11! He's just a kid! He doesn't even know what this is, what we're doing here! Did anyone DO anything?"

"I try not to influence the competition," Geiberger said. "I like to work in the shadows, you understand. Your coach over there—Mr. Raymundo, is it?—finally brought him back to the clubhouse, half an hour after the rest of the kids in his group had finished and signed their scorecards."

"Dewey's the coach," Max said. "But Gabe's playing partner! The other kids in his foursome—didn't they try to do anything to help?"

Geiberger said nothing as he looked across the room at a frumpy kid dressed in green slacks and a white shirt.

Max was there in an instant.

"Did you play with Gabe Buras?"

"Who are you?" The kid looked so smug, so accusatory, with his fat, red face and stubby, uneven teeth.

"Did you play with Gabe Buras?" Max said again. For some reason having to say it twice made him even angrier. "The boy in the white knit cap who wandered over to the glider port on 18?"

Max pointed to Gabe, who was still wandering around the room. The kid followed Max's gaze.

"Who, THAT retard? Yeah, I played with him. What the heck is wrong with that—"

But he never finished the thought.

Maybe if Max had eaten more at breakfast, or Dewey had been there to remind him of his better instincts, to remind him that he was the coach and that it was his job to rise above it, then it's conceivable he could have checked himself. But it all happened too quickly.

In an instant they were on the ground, Max on top, his fists firing like pistons at the fat boy's wet lips and yellow teeth. "That's my brother! That's my brother! That's my brother!"

As if the fat boy in the green slacks really cared, as if he really needed to know. Max raged against Alan Whiting and his stupid car and Mrs. Hickenlooper and her jar of M&M's and checked-out Mr. Raymundo and Max's embarrassing 102 strokes and the awful truth that after all of it the beauty of a simple glider climbing and swooping and diving could rob them of a state title, the first state golf title in Bridge's illustrious history.

It felt cleansing, in a way, to dump all that anger, even like this. There was a purity of purpose, a connection to a time when they were all animals and what did it matter anyway, and Max could now understand the appeal for guys like R.J. and Deke and Rock Bromley as he wailed away, a little slower now, tiring. "That's! My! Bro—"

"Whoa, there, Brock Lesnar!"

Max felt two enormous arms wrapping him up from behind, and opened his eyes to find himself a foot off the ground. He looked over his shoulder at R.J. Hertzenberg, who was barely straining at the effort of the lift. Behind R.J. stood Deke Rawlins, Pete Whiting, Hadley Jackson and an ashen-faced Mr. Raymundo.

"Looks like the referee is calling this one," R.J. said. "Okay if I put you down, Max?"

The fat kid popped to his feet and checked his nose for blood. There was none. "Geez, man," the kid said. "Why didn't you tell me he was your brother?"

"I shouldn't have to!" Max said, flailing his arms and legs.

"Easy!" R.J. said. "I'm going to put you down now. And you're going to chill out, okay?"

Max noticed a crowd had formed around them, including his mother. The room had gone quiet except for Gabe, nonsensically humming Gabe, still wandering in circles.

"Put me down!" Max said. He felt his arms go limp. "Put me down."

R.J. did. Max looked down at his fists. No one had ever mentioned how much it hurt your fists to actually punch someone.

Hadley and Pete looked at him with fear in their eyes, and the sight of them only made the blood rush back up to Max's forehead. They'd bailed on the team. What could be worse than that? "Where have you guys been? We had to go without you."

"The chiropractor!" Deke said. "Isn't that something? I tweaked my back, rolling Whiting's SUV into the river, and so we all went, and it turns out Hadley here is the son of a very good back doctor who works out of his house on Saturdays."

"I'm not even going to ask," Max said.

"So how'd it go?" Hadley said.

"We lost," Max said. "We had a slight attendance problem."

"Not New York State of Mind," said Alex Fisk, whose 74 was easily his best score all year. "He didn't lose. He won the individual title!"

"Nice!" R.J. said as Deke rubbed his lower back.

"Let's hear it for New York State of Mind!" Alex blurted.

The Bridge contingent erupted in a cheer. Max looked over at Ed Hocking, who smiled and shrugged. Hocking looked back up at the score sheet at his giant "65," as if he still couldn't quite believe it was real. Al Geiberger walked over and shook his hand and someone took a picture.

Max made his way over to Gabe, who had finally stopped wandering in circles and was staring into a college football game on the giant TV.

"We're going to find him," Max said, his hands on his knees. "We're going to go find Dewey. And we're going to get you your hat back."

Gabe looked up, his face illuminated by the TV. "No bogeys," he said.

CHAPTER 33

"Just watch it on the freeway onramps," Mr. Raymundo said, handing Sadie the keys to the van. "It doesn't have too many *frijoles* under the hood."

"Got it," Sadie said, taking the keys.

She was old enough to drive without adult supervision now, and the eight of them stood outside the school.

Mr. Raymundo walked away in the direction of the employee parking lot across the street. "*Buenas suerte,*" he said over his shoulder.

"*Gracias*, Mr. Raymundo!" R.J. and Lilly giggled.

"Anybody bring any food?" Max said. "We might be a while, if he's where I think he is."

R.J., Deke, Pete, Hadley, Susannah and Lilly Robinson said nothing.

"You didn't say to bring food," Lilly said.

"Okay, we'll hit a Maverik station somewhere," Max said. "And we're going to have to swing by my house and get Gabe."

He still wasn't sure how he was going to explain that one to his parents.

It was still light out as they piled into the van. Most of the team had gone home, and Max had told Hocking to go celebrate his victory. Alex had come in 10th place individually, and Idaho Falls had won the team title. Bridge had finished a disappointing 14th.

Sadie turned the ignition and they started off with a lurch. "Sorry," she said.

"Oh, great," said Lilly. "This again."

"It's okay," Sadie said. "Don't worry, I'll figure it out as we go. Is it safe to assume everybody is paid up on their insurance?"

It was a short drive to the Grandview Motel. Sadie nosed the van into the parking lot, at the edge of which was a man who looked to be in his twenties with a big belly, droopy-thin mustache, and a tank top that had once been white. He was manning a smoking gas grill, the top up, but with only one hot dog and one hamburger.

"Evening!" Max said, piling out of the front passenger seat.

The guy nodded, raised his spatula.

"I wondered if we might find my friend Dewey here," Max said. "Dewey Tomlinson? He's been missing since this morning."

The guy nodded toward an open door. "That's his room. I've been waiting for him to come back, but I suppose I can close it now. The way it looks in there I don't suppose he's comin' back. Nice van."

"Thanks," Max said. He looked back at their big, brown ride, and Deke, R.J., Susannah and Sadie piling out onto the blacktop and closing the van doors behind them.

Max looked back at the smoking barbecue. "You mind if we have a look around? See if he forgot anything?"

"Didn't even ask for his deposit back," the mustachioed guy said. "Be my guest. Watch the floor—seems he had a little accident with the mirror."

Dewey's room smelled like cigarettes. There was an empty pizza box. Some pennies on the dresser. A can of Lemon Pledge. A broken mirror and the shattered remains of a cell phone. Some of the shrapnel had come to rest atop the giant "Gru" head in the corner, left over from Halloween.

"I think I figured out why he's not returning my messages," Max said.

"Max."

"Yeah?"

Sadie came out of the bathroom and held up a die-cast Star Wars TIE Fighter, Max's present to Dewey and Gabe.

"What's that thing?" Susannah said.

"Star Wars deal," Deke said. He reached down for something on the dresser and held up a crumpled pack of Pall Malls. "I thought he quit smoking."

"He did," Sadie said. "But it didn't last. Apparently his life got a little stressful in recent weeks. I can't imagine why."

"Bring the tie fighter," Max told his sister. "And let's get out of here."

They piled back into the van, and Max looked down at the beastly vessel's center console, with its cup holders. He hadn't even brought a water bottle.

"I know where he is," he said, loud enough for only Sadie to hear. "And it's going to be a long ride."

✿ ✿ ✿

An hour later they were on the road, pointed east, Gabe asleep on the floor at the feet of the crew in the first row of seats.

"I don't get it," Lilly said. "Why don't we just call him or whatever?"

"Because he literally blew up his cell phone," Max said. "I saw it back at the Grandview. It's in a million pieces."

"Please say it's a Galaxy," Susannah said.

"Why?" Max asked.

"He turned it into Galaxy dust," Susannah said. "Right? Galaxy dust?"

"Yeah," Max said.

Getting Gabe out of the house had been surprisingly easy. He'd been in such a state all afternoon their mother was exhausted, and their father hadn't come back from work yet, and seeing as how car travel often put him at ease, and how Max said they were only going to drive around some and look for Dewey, whose absence had triggered Gabe's meltdown after all, she'd reluctantly let him go.

Max hadn't told her they planned to look for Dewey in Jackson, Wyoming, six hours away.

"Dewey's a climber," Max said to everyone in the van. "He's been planning to climb the Grand Teton for—well, for ever since I've known him. He's been practically living at REI, checking out climbing photos online, and testing G.O.R.P. recipes. I'm telling you the man is headed to Jackson, if he's not already there."

Lilly stopped running her fingers through R.J.'s hair. "We're driving all the way to, like, Wyoming? How long is that?"

"Six hours," Max said.

"Oh, my God," Lilly said. "I should have brought my script."

"Susannah," Max said, looking back at his girlfriend over his left shoulder. "You know the script. *Groundhog Day*? Can you run lines with Lilly?

Sadie would do it but she's driving."

"Just not the ice sculpture part," Susannah said, flashing Max a suggestive smile that got his heart pumping.

The van was loaded down with an obscene amount of gear, all of it from the Maverik service station by the Interstate, all paid for with Alan Whiting's credit card, which Pete said his dad had given him "for emergencies." They had rope, flares, an orange traffic cone, two orange hunting vests for R.J. and Deke, jerky, chips, soda, candy bars, four giant jugs of water, a bag of unpopped, Orville Redenbacher popcorn.

"Hey," Hadley said from the second row. "Who bought the popcorn? And what are we supposed to do with it, cook it in the muffler?"

"Hey, yourself!" Lilly said. "I just like popcorn, okay? I forgot we didn't have, like, the hot-air thingie, okay?"

Max laughed. Someone had found Gabe's cap on the course, probably on the 18th fairway next to the glider port, which put Max in a slightly better mood. But he became positively ebullient when the others told him how they'd spent the morning rolling Alan Whiting's stupid U.S. Open-logoed car into the Boise River.

"Pete!" Max said loudly, projecting his voice over the van's noisy, old engine and into the second row of bench seating, where Pete Whiting was eating a bag of Fritos. "You rolled your own dad's car?"

Pete smiled. "Yeah. Felt good, too."

Max tried to digest the news: Pete Whiting was on his side—or on Dewey's side, at least. But was he really?

"Pete," Max said.

"Yeah," Pete said again.

"Your dad," Max said. "The newspaper deal—the truth about Dewey's past. Tell me you didn't tell your dad. Please tell me…"

"God, no!" Pete said. "I asked him how he found out because I was pretty goddamned curious myself, but he wasn't feeling all that chatty with his car bobbing along down the river, so I asked my mom. Turns out my dad plays golf with Oliver Johnson, the lawyer dude, who works with, among his other clients—"

"The school district," Max said.

"Yep," Pete said.

Mr. Johnson. The suit. So that was it then. Never trust a lawyer. "Well, Dewey thanks you," Max said.

"For what?"

"For taking his side," Max said. He thought about adding something, but then decided against it, but then thought what the hell, just put it out there. "I wish you'd taken my side in the fall."

The van got quiet.

"You don't know?" Hadley said. "You don't know who cast the other vote in your favor?"

Max shook his head. "Nope."

"Tell him," Hadley said, turning to Pete.

"I did," Pete said.

Max felt the hair on the back of neck stand up. "But you—"

"I just delivered the message," Pete said. "I didn't try to vote you off the team. You can thank Alex and Don and Phil for that." He paused, looked through the van windows at the setting sun.

Pete Whiting was on Dewey's side *and* on Max's side. Could it be? Max trusted Hadley, at least. This day was getting weirder by the minute. Max was exhausted.

He woke up as they slowly crawled through Idaho Falls, and as the van passed a bar Max saw that someone had already adjusted the marquee out front to reflect the day's events: CONGRATS I.F.H.S. TIGERS – STATE GOLF CHAMPS 2015!

They rolled into Jackson just a little after 1 a.m., and Max blinked his eyes in an effort to get used to the dark. He had made up a list of climbing guides in the area, the top 10 as listed on Google, but he'd forgotten to check hotel prices and availability. He had six text messages on his phone from his father, and two from his mother. He looked into the back seat, everyone smooshed up against each other like a pile of puppies. Susannah was asleep against the window, her hair having fallen over her nose and mouth.

"I've gotta get some coffee," Deke said. He had taken over for Sadie behind the wheel while Max slept.

Max heard Gabe stirring. Great. Now his little brother was waking up. He never woke up. If there was one thing Gabe could be relied on for it was sleeping through the night. Max turned his neck hard to the left, eying the floor. Yes, Gabe was definitely waking up.

He never wakes up. So why now, and while sleeping above the gentle hum of a car engine, no less? In his mind Max saw a montage of the previous fall, Dewey, the tow truck, Gabe, speech pathologist Cynthia, and bio-harmonic convergence. Gabe sat up, suddenly wide-awake.

"Pull in here," Max said.

"It's just a supermarket," Deke said.

"Look at the sign!" Max said, his heart racing. "There's a Starbucks inside!"

"Okay, okay, calm down." Deke steered the van into the parking lot, right past a tall man holding a cardboard sign—too slow to miss him, but not slow enough to pay him.

"Back up," Max said.

"What?" Deke said. "C'mon, Max. Those guys are scammers."

Gabe was humming loudly, standing in the back of the van and staring out the window. He banged on the glass, first softly but then increasingly hard as the others emerged from their sleep.

"Back up," Max said again. "Please back up."

Deke did as told, and Max looked over him at Dewey Tomlinson outside the driver's side window. He was wearing an orange, long-sleeved shirt and holding a cardboard sign: "LIFE BLOWN TO BITS. ANYTHING HELPS."

"Holy Moses," Deke said. "We found him. How did we find him?"

Dewey let his hand fall so his sign grazed the side of his leg. He looked up at the sky, down at his feet, back at the van. He looked back in the direction of the supermarket.

Max opened the door to get out.

"I'm going to park," Deke said.

"Okay." Max shut the van door. "Wake up Sadie and tell her to call our folks, okay? They're going to be pulling their hair out. And tell her to call Cynthia."

"Who's Cynthia?"

"Dewey's girlfriend."

Deke looked at Dewey through his open window. "Yeaaaaah, Dewey!

CHAPTER THIRTY THREE

How's it goin', my man? What are you doin' out here? Nice sign!"

Deke took his foot off the brake and pulled to a stop diagonally across two parking spaces. There were only about four or five cars in the whole lot.

Max stood in front of Dewey now, Dewey still with the mountaineering boots, and the same old pair of cut-off khaki shorts Max had seen a million times before. He was the same Dewey who had been celebrating his birthday with Gabe just that morning in Boise, only now he was in Jackson, Wyoming, six hours away. Panhandling. He tried to ignore Max, avoiding eye contact.

"What are you doing?" Max said.

Dewey finally broke off his thousand-yard stare into nothing and looked down at Max, his old video poker wingman, sometime golf buddy and occasional confidant on matters of the heart.

"What's it look like I'm doing? I'm working." Dewey thought for a moment. "Well, some people wouldn't call it working, but it's competitive."

"Competitive?"

"Yeah," Dewey said. "Guy across the parking lot, he's gone for the night now, but he's got this whole spiel about how he's from Yorba Linda, California, and he's here with his wife and five kids and his car ran out of gas and they need money to fill it up. Guy's been killing me! Or maybe it's San Ysidro. It's got a 'Y' in it. He probably changes it up."

Max looked at his watch, then up at Dewey. "It's one o'clock in the morning."

"Yeah! I got the lot to myself!"

"Uh," Max said. "Is that a good thing? No people here." He could tell Dewey was trying to convince himself of something. Max continued, "You're here to climb the Grand?"

"Yeah! How'd you know?"

"You've only been talking about it all school year."

"Oh," Dewey said.

"Shouldn't you be at, like, base camp or something and not in an Albertsons parking lot?"

"Yeah, but it turns out a guided ascent is a little more than I thought," Dewey said. "And I blew a lot more than I planned to on golf clubs. And the Crown Vic needed a new alternator. I'm running a bit low on funds."

"I thought you had money. From Jackpot?"

"Turns out I spent most of it," Dewey said.

"You mean you spent it all on me and Gabe."

"Aw, not all of it. I got no regrets, it's all good—just a temporary setback."

"Oh!" Dewey added, as if he'd just remembered. "How'd you guys do today?"

"Um, not very well," Max said. "We finished 14th due to an attendance problem. Suffice it to say I played, and Gabe played, and I shot a 102. Gabe didn't record a score, so we had to use mine, which is why we lost. And I got in my first fight."

"Yikes," Dewey said. "Well, you just haven't practiced enough. Keep at it—the golf—not the fighting. You'll have to tell me about that. How'd Gabe do?"

"He didn't record a score, Dewey."

Dewey's face registered the fact that he'd just asked a question he shouldn't have because he had a role in all of this, how a little boy who had had *trouble maintaining stability in his life* had finally come into himself and then, just as quickly, fallen apart.

"He needs you," Max said. "He crashed, went back to Gabe Land. He wandered over to the glider port and made himself at home and never even finished the 18th hole."

Deke cleared his throat. "Um, we rolled Pete's dad's Lexus into the river. I just thought you should know. That was a pretty crappy thing he put in the paper."

Dewey brightened. "No kidding?"

"I didn't have anything to do with it," Max said. "I was busy with team stuff, but apparently there was a sort of flash mob organized by Sadie, who is asleep over there in the van, to dispense a little vigilante justice."

"Hey, thanks!" Dewey said.

"Don't mention it," Deke said, rubbing his shoulder. "It was a good workout."

"Gabe needs you," Max said again.

"I'm not wanted there," Dewey said. "You saw the paper this morning."

"That's just one guy!" Max said. "Alan Whiting is crazy. No one takes him seriously, not even his kid. Pete helped roll the Lexus into the river this morning!"

"He did? Pete did that?"

"Yeah!" Max said. "And he's here! Deke! Go get Pete!"

"He's asleep in the van," Deke said.

"He's asleep in the van!" Max said. "You'll have to believe me. Or go over there and look, if you want. I think everyone is asleep."

Dewey squinted as he appraised the van from afar. "How many you got in there?"

"Seven," Max said. "Or eight, sorry. I think."

He'd almost forgotten Gabe.

"You forgot this," Max said, reaching into his jacket pocket and producing a die-cast Star Wars TIE Fighter with six-sided wings. "I found it on your bathroom sink."

Dewey's eyes got shiny, but he hung on, his face making a few weird contortions to keep it together as he took the TIE fighter out of Max's hands. But then there was a shutting of a door, and all three men looked over at sleepy-eyed Gabe, newly 11, shuffling toward them.

His hair was mussed, and he was drowning in his too-big Star Wars pajamas, the bottoms dragging along the pebble-strewn parking lot. The lights in the parking lot seemed to shine with a new purpose now, and even Deke looked up at them.

Gabe stopped in front of Dewey and smiled. The boy's hand held his tiny TIE fighter, which he began to make fly in great rises and dips and loop-de-loops, and Dewey's tiny toy TIE fighter and cardboard sign clattered to the pavement. He dropped his head and he began to cry, silently at first but then his lungs gasped for air and he began making great, messy sobs.

"You have to come back," Max said softly. "You have to teach Gabe how to ride a bike."

Dewey's red-rimmed eyes were still leaking tears, and he dabbed them with his sleeves. He looked over at Deke, who was making his way toward Albertsons, maybe for a cup of coffee, and then at Gabe and Max. Dewey got his breathing under control. "You got into a fight?"

"Yeah," Max said.

"Did you win?"

"I'll tell you about it later."

Gabe pulled his rumpled cap out of the crook of his arm and placed it atop his head, and Dewey looked down at him and lost it all over again, shoulders heaving, body quaking. "Argh!" he said. "Get it together!"

"You have to come back," Max said again. "You have to come home. To Boise."

Dewey looked down at the cardboard sign on the ground, its black, indelible ink message face up—LIFE BLOWN TO BITS—and then back at Max and Gabe as he wiped his nose on his shirtsleeve. "You don't have a paper towel or anything, do you?" Dewey laughed and shook his head, dabbing at his eyes now. "I'm a mess."

"We've got some in the van."

Dewey looked across the parking lot at the official vehicle of the Bridge golf team, 14th best in the state.

"Come on," Max said, hooking him by the arm.

"Yeah," Gabe said, hooking the big man's other arm. "Come into our van."

Dewey did.

This book would not have been possible without the patience of my wife, Ellen, and daughter, Lucy. I love you both. For the early reads I'm indebted to Michelle Kuchuk, Emily Bunker, Jane Bunker and Mason Morfit. To Christian Winn and everyone at Writers Write, Amanda Turner and the rest of the gang at Writers Rendezvous, fearless Treasure Valley NaNo WriMo leader Christy Hovey, and Darren Sand—thank you. Many thanks also to my editor Anna McHargue, biking buddy and big picture guy Mark Russell, and the rest of the Elevate team. I also would like to thank both Evan Rothman for the early read and my fearless leader at Golf Magazine, David Clarke.

elevate
publishing

A strategic publisher empowering authors to strengthen their brand.

Visit Elevate Publishing for our latest offerings.
www.elevatepub.com

NO TREES WERE HARMED
IN THE MAKING OF THIS BOOK

OK, so a few
did need to make the ultimate sacrifice.

In order to steward our environment,
    we are partnering with *Plant With Purpose*, to plant
a tree for every tree that paid the price for the printing of
    this book.

PLANT WITH PURPOSE

www.plantwithpurpose.org

go to www.elevatepub.com/about to learn more